Plumb
Crazy

Plumb Crazy

Cece Barlow

Caney
Creek
Books

This is a work of fiction. All incidents, dialogue, and characters are products of the author's imagination and are not to be construed as real. The author makes no claims to, but wholly acknowledges the trademarked status and trademark owners of all wordmarks mentioned in this work of fiction. In all other respects, any resemblance to persons living or dead, business establishments, events or local is entirely coincidental.

DEDICATION

For Dayna, Georgia, Elissa, and Jubilee

The only things you need
to know about plumbing:
Shit don't run uphill
and payday is on Friday.

– Mr. Bob, master plumber

1 BYOB

Come out for the Belling High School reunion. Set ups for BYOB.

The invitation arrived by mail. Her five year class reunion.

Elva could hardly believe it had been five years. It was amazing how fast time burned up in a puff of college classes, summer jobs, and road trips to sci-fi conventions (her guilty pleasure). A return to high school seemed like a waste of time, but then Shay had called and after that, Margarett. Her best friends, the Loser Girls, a name born of junior high foolishness—they wanted to reunite, and she couldn't say no.

She put out the fifty dollars for the reunion boat ride on Lake Conroe, along with barbeque and country western dancing. Next, she'd shopped for a new dress since the planning committee insisted that everyone wear formals.

"Elva Presley, are you ready?" Her grandmother, Nonny, was watching TV.

Elva headed into the living room. "Do you like my outfit?" she asked, spinning in a fuchsia mini with sparkly shoulder straps. She kicked out a cowgirl boot decorated with swirled embroidery.

"Oh, Elva Presley, you look so much like your mama did," Nonny said.

Elva laughed. She was all generous curves, and her mama had been model thin.

Papaw came out of the bathroom. "Elva, do you have enough gas money for tonight?"

"I'm fine. I've got my internship pay. I just need my purse, and then I'll pick up Margarett in Jersey Village. Shay's meeting us at the boat."

Elva glanced around the living room for her clutch purse. She checked in the bedroom. Her sparkly clutch jutted out from under the bed. When she reached down to pick it up, her fingers grazed a rubber-banded stack of paper. Elva hooked the purse over her wrist and picked up the stack. The edges of the sheets were curled, and faded coffee stains blossomed across the cover page.

Her breath caught in her throat when she read the title. "The Death Incident."

She hadn't seen this manuscript since she started college. Her lips curved into her widest smile. It suddenly all seemed like yesterday.

Elva went to her car, a yellow Yaris that she'd paid off herself last summer. She put it in gear and headed to Margarett's. Vivid memories flooded back of Belling High School, a low cinder block building hunkered down in hardscrabble grassland choked by bull nettle and scourged by fire ants. The cafeteria doors were painted mud-coffee to hide the dirt.

Elva recalled those days like they had just happened, the summer after her junior year.

***

She pushed in the cafeteria door for the start of the last day of school.

"Hey, Shay, Margarett." Elva waved at her best friends.

Trapped souls eyed her as she joined her tribe huddled at the table by the window. The wide view of cerulean sky was marred only by the Belling water tower. The hell of high school was almost bearable with such a view.

"Shay, can I have your cinnamon roll?" Elva asked.

"Sure." Shay slid over the gooey roll.

Elva pulled out their current fanfic pages and placed them on the table. It felt good to connect with her tribe. They only had so many minutes to work. Their last day of school had snuck up on them and their junior year was over; the summer allowed for only occasional meet-ups at Sonic Drive-in's Happy Hour.

"We've got to focus," Elva said. "Our time is *sooo* … ermph … limited." Her words were gummed up with cinnamony dough. "In the last scene, Spock escaped the Romulans' death trap and saved his long lost daughter."

"So what happens next?" Margarett asked, tweaking her softball-sized hair bun.

"Shouldn't it be his sister?" Shay asked. "Spock's young and, you know, hot."

"That's revisionist Trek!" Elva shook their pages at her friend. "No Abrams reboot for us. Omigod, do you want to create another *Enterprise* disaster!"

"Shay, Elva's right," Margarett said. "Spock must save his daughter. It's logical."

Elva took another bite of roll. "Margo, can I have your milk?"

"Sure." Margarett slid her carton to Elva, who took a noisy slurp.

"OK … OK." Shay said. "Spock's gonna save his daughter. I get it, but before we go on, listen to this!" She opened her prized Coach bag from the Goodwill and turned on her cell phone. "It's a new ring tone." A jazzy *Star Trek* riff played.

So awesome, but sigh, with no cell phone, no cable, no modern conveniences, Elva tried to survive on the ancient technologies of a boxy desktop computer and a landline. Visions of posting *Star Trek* fanfic stories bubbled within her—electric dreams of upgrades—a Mac, DSL, and a cell phone with unlimited text messaging.

"Hey, heifers!" A tampon soaked in ketchup splatted across their table and stopped in a crack.

It was thrown by Kyle, better known as "the student most likely to go postal," even lower on the food chain of Hell than Elva and her friends.

Shay shot Kyle an angry glare but didn't say anything. Margarett lifted a tray like she was raising shields.

"Kyle, are you an alien life form?" Elva stood up. "You better stay away from our space or else!"

"What are you planning to do?" Kyle asked.

"Do you really want to find out?" Elva's crazy was legendary at Belling High; surviving Hell did things like that to you. She stamped her foot at him, and he slunk off like the coward he was. She tossed the tampon in the trash.

"Let's get to work, gals." Elva took her seat and reshuffled their pages.

"Kyle's kinda cute," Margarett whispered. "Do you think he likes me?" Margarett had tribble-like intelligence, but like tribbles she was loveable anyway.

"He just called us cows and threw a tampon at us," Shay said. "Rapist? Maybe. Boyfriend? Never."

"Well, I'm going to pray for him," Margarett said.

"You do that." Elva tapped their pages into a neat stack. "Back to our fanfic, Loser Girls. Remember, it's our glue, our ticket out of nowhere, our deliverance from Hell. We can't give in to Kyle's bad karma."

"Isn't karma something to do with tarot cards?" Margarett asked. "That's of the devil."

"Margarett, karma isn't of the devil. The devil is religious phoniness." Elva let her words fly. "The devil is Shay's drunken mother. The devil is

11

'golden sponge cake with creamy filling', never karma."

"What's religious phoniness?" Margarett's lip trembled. She was always sure God was about to strike her down.

"Not you. But think about all the killing and wars because of religion. That's what I'm talking about." Elva spoke softly. Margarett was extra mired in religious nonsense, and shoehorning her out was a delicate process.

"Elva's right about the devil," Shay said. "She's trying to help us rise up, and part of that is telling us the truth."

Elva leaned in. "I'm getting us on the road to Somewhere if it's the only thing I ever do."

"Speaking of Somewhere," Shay said. "What are you doing this summer?"

"What do you mean?" Elva asked.

"Here's the deal. I got a job."

Elva was totally silent. Margarett took a sharp breath. Shay had a job. They weren't going to spend the summer munching stale bags of Fritos from the food bank. Elva lifted an eyebrow, Spock-like. *Fascinating.*

"What are you doing?" Elva asked.

"I'm a waitress at Don's Truck Stop."

"No way," Elva said. It was too fantastic. Shay was going to work in a restaurant with real people.

"They need another girl," Shay said. "It pays a couple of dollars an hour plus tips."

To boldly go where no—

"I got a job, too." Margarett added in a small

voice. "My grandmother knows the shift lead at the Wal-Mart Supercenter. I'm helping at the deli counter for minimum wage."

Elva dropped her notebook and pushed away from the table. It was too much. "Dear God, I wish I had a job!"

"Apply at Don's," Shay said. "All you need is parental permission."

"I don't even have a beater. How would I get into town?" A bubble of pain rose in Elva's belly. Shay and Margarett had jobs, dang it.

"Don's isn't too far to walk," Margarett said.

Elva refrained from rolling her eyes. Margarett never had to walk anywhere because she could always get a ride from one of her umpteen relatives.

"Ask your Papaw for permission." Shay pressed. "You've got to do it. You can't drive into Houston, and I think this is the only job left in Belling."

Shay was right about that. Belling was a black hole when it came to jobs. Elva smoothed out their fanfic pages. "OK, I'll ask Papaw. I promise." She crossed her heart. "But, come on. Let's get to work. Precious fanfic time is a wasting."

They finished the scene by the time the lunch bell rang. On the way to class, Elva leaned against her locker. How would she ever get a job?

She whispered her calming mantra. She'd wikied mantras at the library.

"Being poor sucks. Accepting it is the pathway of peace."

Sacred words have power.

And those sacred words carried her through the rest of the day. When she climbed aboard her bus to go home, waves of little kids' screams and random cursing followed her to her goal—the rear seats—the domain of the high schoolers. Elva plopped onto the backseat and put her feet on the one in front of her. A day was coming when she would never ride a bus again, and, dear God, she was waiting for that day like people waiting for the Rapture when Christ gathered the believers into heaven.

The seat next to her squeaked loudly, and Elva edged toward the window. Dylan and Jolie were seriously making out. Their baby screamed in the car seat in front of them, and both ignored the sound. Belling High School's daycare had twenty babies in it, though everybody knew that condoms were available in the nurse's office. *Star Trek* characters seemed to have the same problem. Almost every major one had a love child somewhere.

That night Elva did what any Loser Girl of the Universe would do. She scrambled up her nerve and asked her papaw if she could work at Don's Truck Stop.

"Papaw, my friend Shay has a job at Don's, and they're looking for another waitress."

"No dang granddaughter of mine is working at a dang truck stop. It ain't good for you. It ain't good for nobody." Deep creases formed on his weathered forehead. "Do you know men pinch girls' butts at truck stops?"

14

If only she could be so lucky to get her oh so ample butt pinched at a truck stop, but there was no arguing with Papaw. Once he set his mind, he never changed it, come hell or high water. Elva stamped into the bathroom and plopped down on the classic elongated Porcher toilet. She picked at the duct tape surrounding the bathtub faucet and then spun the escutcheon on the water inlet.

No slice in the pie of life for her. Fate loomed: giant pants, minimum wage, and no boyfriends. Yet, deep beneath her layers of vinegary resignation were hovering things. They burned— these smoldering embers—thoughts of junior-sized pants, a living wage, and a smoking hot boyfriend.

"Get out of that dang bathroom!" Papaw beat on the door.

"I will when I'm good and ready."

A job like Don's could change her whole life. Papaw was so freaking country. How was she to jumpstart her life without money? Railing at Papaw seemed better than facing the plain truth— she didn't have the nerve to go against him and do what she wanted anyway. Her yellow-bellied coward self would have sat on the toilet all night if the smell of frying hamburger hadn't wafted under the bathroom door. Heck. No fit was worth missing supper.

In the kitchen, Papaw fried ground beef and had a box of Hamburger Helper open. He'd put on a record, and Elvis's "All Shook Up" crackled from ancient speakers. He dumped noodles into the skillet.

"You want work? I've got you work." He placed his hands on the sides of his barrel belly. "You should help me this summer. You can hire out with Carus Residential and Industrial as a plumber's helper."

Like hell.

"Gal, I just talked to Mr. Bob. He owes me a big favor, so he'll pay you a contract wage of $17.13 an hour with time and half for overtime. Under the table, mind you, with no cut for Uncle Sam."

$17.13 an hour? Elva took a slow cleansing breath. There was no way she could turn down that much money. No way.

She—an ultimate Loser Girl—answered, "OK, Papaw."

Elva was going to be a plumber gal, holy snappin'.

2 DANG KIDS

Early the next morning, Elva woke to pitiful crying. Dang kids. Saturday was her day to sleep in, but that wasn't in her cards. Papaw was long gone, and someone had to take care of the goats.

"Nonny, are you planning to feed the kids?" Elva called across the small house.

"In a few minutes," her grandmother groaned.

Elva stumbled into the bathroom and washed her face. She slopped on moisturizer but didn't really need it; her peaches and cream complexion was one of her best features. Her wide-set eyes stood out, too. They changed color with whatever she wore. She stuck out her tongue at her slacker features—her upturned nose, too round face, and regrettable double chin.

Her thoughts drifted back to the worry of

plumbing as she brushed her teeth. Would she have to slog around in sewage? Would her butt crack ever show? She pulled up her pants with an extra tug. Fretting wasn't helping anything. She spat out her toothpaste and wiped her face.

"Here's breakfast." Nonny's girth filled the doorway. She clutched a box of expired honey buns to her chartreuse housecoat.

Honey buns. Elva had a particular weakness for honey buns.

The babies bleated crazily with hunger now. "Will you feed the kids? I'm just not up to it," Nonny said, handing Elva the box.

The lure of the honey buns overwhelmed her.

"I'll take care of them, Nonny." Elva took two buns.

"That's my good girl." Nonny's bare feet slapped against the floor as she waddled back to her bedroom.

Elva wanted to yell, "Take care of your own freaking goats!" Instead, she reached for a third honey bun. The soft sweetness of each bite melted in her mouth.

In the kitchen, she placed three giant plastic Coke bottles in the sink and heated water to steaming. Mixing in the formula produced a sickly sweet smell, gag worthy. She filled the bottles and headed to the breezeway at the back of the house.

Three Alpine kids, chocolaty brown with white blazes down their faces and the size of long-legged house cats, clamored on the steps.

"Maaa, maa." Scabbed heads rammed against her legs. The babies' horns had been polled, burned off a few days back.

She sank down on the steps. The concrete hadn't yet absorbed the humid Texas heat. Tiny hooves tapped against her shoulders as the nameless babies clamored for their bottles.

"Hold on, I've got what y'all need," she crooned. The Alpines butted at her legs. Elva held tight to the bottles. "Maybe you shouldn't be so eager, guys."

She pulled a goat into her lap. Goats were one of Nonny's big ideas to make spare cash. The thought of these babies butchered sent shivers down Elva's spine.

"Maaa, maaa," the baby in her lap cried.

"Do you want to hear the feeding story again?" Elva held a bottle to the crying baby's mouth, and it began sucking vigorously. The other two butted her sides, anxious for their bottles too.

"The story starts with your mama. She died giving you life."

The warm goat snuggled in her lap. Its body quivered.

"The same thing happened to my mama. Your mama dying reminded Nonny of Willa Jo too much."

Thankfully, the goats would never understand how things broke people forever. The pain of Willa Jo's death left Nonny loving Elva with a kind of love that had all kinds of sharp pieces, like shattered glass.

"My mama was a cheerleader." Elva shifted on the steps and went on with her story. "A gal going someplace until she hooked up with a truck driver from Wichita. He knocked her up and cut out of town. No one ever heard from him again."

The baby goat stopped sucking on its bottle and bleated.

"Yeah, he deserved a voodoo curse for not ever giving a whit about me."

The baby goat sneezed, shaking its head.

"But I decided to not let his stupidity taint all of my possibility."

The first goat was finished nursing, and she picked up the next one. Elva sighed. Not having a dad sucked, but it was even worse to be the reason one of the bright shining stars of Belling, Texas, didn't go on with her life. It was a special place in Hell. Her mom would have put Belling on the map. She might have been a beauty queen. Everybody said so. The folks in Belling thought of Elva as the exact opposite, an infinite well of disappointment. Only Nonny had ever hoped against hope. She'd named Elva after the biggest star in her universe—Elvis Presley.

So far none of that star power had rubbed off.

The bottle emptied with the sharp cracking sound of the plastic collapsing inward. Elva began to feed the last baby goat. When its bottle was empty, she let it stumble to join the others in the makeshift yard fenced with rusty chicken wire off the breezeway. The enormous responsibility of keeping the goats alive weighed on her like river stones piled on her chest. She went back in the house and dumped the bottles in the sink.

An ominous growl came from her stomach.

She fried two slices of bologna and ate them with a half carton of cottage cheese. She watched a boring Spanish soap, but soon dragged the phone outside to talk to her friends. Papaw wouldn't have a cordless. He believed they caused brainwaves to mess up. Nonny had read about the danger in *The Globe*, *The Star*, and *The National Inquirer*, her holy trinity of truth. Elva tugged at the tangled cord and grunted. Right after she bought a decent laptop, she'd spring for a cell phone with her plumbing cash. She punched in Shay's number. The phone rang five times before a slurred voice answered.

"I hope to God this is important!" Shay's ma was drunk again and before noon.

"May I speak to Shay?" Elva asked.

"What the hell are you doing calling the house at this hour?"

"Is Shay around?" Elva tried again.

"She's working up at the damn truck stop all weekend," her mother said. The line clicked and the phone went dead.

Elva didn't try to call Margarett. Her phone had been temporarily disconnected three months ago. Anyway, they were meeting tomorrow at the Sonic Drive-In. Elva's news about a job would just have to wait until then.

"Guys," Elva said to the kids. "How about a walk?"

She fumbled with the screen door and reached inside the house for her worn Converse tennis shoes. Elva didn't put them on, but walked barefoot into the yard.

"This will only take a minute," she said to the goats and folded her hands in prayer. She took a breath and turned her face toward the sun, connecting with its light. Her yoga practice temporarily lifted her out of survival mode and up into a stratosphere of infinite possibilities. For a brief moment she was more—Elva Presley Hicks, the rising sun, spreading out and warming the earth. She exhaled and folded into child's pose, smiling as one of the goats nibbled her ear.

She lifted off the ground on all fours and pushed into downward facing dog. One goat nuzzled her stomach as her body formed the requisite v. The stretch reached from her fingers, to her spine, and all the way down to her toes. She breathed in, living in this instant. Her concentration broke when one of the goats climbed her legs to stand on her bottom, sticking up in the air.

"Watch out," she said, stepping forward with one foot, then the other. The goat leaped gracefully to the ground. Elva raised her hands to the sky, fully recognizing that all living things consist of condensed sunlight. At least that's what her *Yoga for Dummies* book had said to do.

"I'm ready now, guys."

Elva pulled on her shoes and strolled down the blacktop road with the kids following. At the corner was a grouping of white crosses. She touched a cross and spoke to the goats. "A carload of people died on this corner. One was Margarett's cousin."

The kids wobbled around on white sock legs. Their chocolate coats gleamed in the sunlight. Elva acknowledged the deep connection between them. The goats, like her, brimmed full of promise and hope, but had only a wing and a prayer to find their best life. She dreamed of writing *Trek* novels and doing signings in Vegas at *Trek* conventions, and she dreamed of getting out of giant pants. She didn't know what goats dreamed about, but they deserved the chance to live their dreams too.

She knelt down. One of the babies placed its tiny hooves on her shoulder. Another chewed on her hair.

"Y'all will live long and prosper. I promise."

She settled back on her haunches. Saving the goats would be a powerful sign, a portent of the tide turning. She'd buck destiny and with goat-saving karma rocket out of small town hell.

So she named the goats, swinging toward her favorite original *Trek* trio, the medical staff. It was a holy moment like baptizing a baby. She touched her nose to the first kid.

"You're Dr. Leonard 'Bones' McCoy."

She touched the next one's silky ears. "You're Dr. M'Benga."

Last she rubbed her face against the remaining kid's coarse chocolate coat. "You're Nurse Christine Chapel."

And it was done.

She returned home and penned the kids. Papaw's truck was parked by the house. Inside, she checked the Elvis clock with swinging legs by the fridge. There was more than enough time for a trip to the library. The TV blared in the living room, and Nonny propped her feet up on the coffee table. Papaw snored like a chainsaw in the bedroom.

"Nonny, drive with me to the library," Elva begged. She only had a learner's permit in her pocketbook. There just wasn't enough money for the independent driving upgrade.

"I'm feeling puny." Nonny said, refusing to budge.

No new books. Intolerable.

The library was Elva's portal to the universe. Since her last online check at the Belling Public Library her blog had recorded ninety hits, though most came from Shay with a few from spammers. Still, eight people were waiting in the wings for her hot debut in the Trekkie fandom universe. She had one story almost—*almost*—ready for her visionary Internet splash-down. Up to this point, she'd only posted *about* her brilliant stories on her blog. The world had to be readied for her brand of powerful storytelling.

Elva's day dribbled on. She took a nap and then fed the kids again. After supper, Papaw and Nonny watched a murder mystery on the TV. Elva knew who did it in five minutes and spent the rest of the evening wrestling with making Spock's daughter seem authentic.

Around midnight, Elva heard a knock at the door.

"Who is it," Elva asked.

"Me, Shay."

"Come on in." Elva opened the door.

Shay smelled of burnt grease and menthol cigarette smoke. "Mama threw me out."

"Did you walk here all the way from Don's?"

Shay nodded. "I didn't have a ride. Mama's too drunk to see what her boyfriend Lenny Dean is up to. His eyes follow me everywhere. You know, connected to my boobs and ass, and then he sticks out his tongue and wiggles it at me." Shay stuck her finger in her throat and feigned vomiting. "He groped me before work, and I kicked him in the balls. He told Mama I was wiling him. Then she threw me out."

Elva sighed. Nonny and Papaw always let Shay stay until things cooled down at home. Her friend lived under a wild squall over the Gulf, and all the Universe had given her was a rickety rowboat. Dang Universe. "I'll get you a sheet. You can sleep on the couch. Why don't you hop in the shower while I make your bed?"

Shay headed to the bathroom while Elva saved her files and powered down her computer for the night. Then she pulled the sheet off her bed to use on the couch.

"Can I put my uniform in the washer?" Shay toweled her hair as she came out of the bathroom.

"Sure." Elva nodded, smoothing the sheet over the cushions. "How's working at the truck stop?"

"Pretty good. I made forty-five dollars in tips."

"Omigod!" Elva pretended to faint into a chair.

"I'm buying jeans at the mall instead of Wal-Mart."

"Seriously, you could save up and buy a pair from Urban Outfitters." Elva sat up and crossed her legs.

"I wish you could work with me," Shay said.

"It's all right," Elva said. "I got a job, too."

"You did?" Shay exclaimed. "Where? When?"

"I plan to work at Carus Industrial and Residential as a plumber's helper for $17.13 an hour." Elva said it perfectly calmly.

"That's fantastic. When do you start?"

"On Monday."

"Are you sure you don't want to work at Don's?" Shay asked. "It's good money there, too."

"Nope, I'm set on plumbing." Elva glanced down at her thick thighs. Their size 22 magnificence would not likely garner the kind of tips that Shay received. As a bonus, Shay's eyes were bluebonnet blue and her brown hair had blonde streaks.

"At least you'll have money," Shay said. "We can go to the mall in a couple of weeks. Or save up and go to a real live *Star Trek* convention. Maybe we'd meet some of the cast members."

"I've always wanted to go to an open read for fanfic and share our story," Elva said.

"Yeah, awesome," Shay said and then sighed. "The new Captain Kirk is okay, but old Captain Kirk used to be way hotter. I was born at the wrong time."

"I'll print some pages of our story right now," Elva said. "And we could go over them." A trip into fanfic fantasy seemed called for.

"I'd love to do that, Elva." Shay yawned. "But I've got an early shift tomorrow." She pulled the sheet up to her neck and curled up.

"Maybe another time," Elva said.

"OK," Shay murmured. "I'm so sleepy." Her eyes shut and her body gave a flinch. Elva had never met anyone who could fall asleep as fast as Shay. She picked up Shay's uniform and tossed it the washer, and then went back to her room.

Elva wished she was a heavy sleeper and could dive head first into the grace of dream-life. The window AC in the living room didn't cool her room down much. The box fan on her dresser blew at full blast through a damp towel to cool down the air too. Still it was hotter than heck. Elva punched her pillow and prayed she'd have the dream where she was a Star Fleet ensign beaming down for leave on the pleasure planet of Risa.

3 CATFISH KISS

When Elva woke up, she moaned. No dreams.
Waaah! Shay was already up and ironing her
uniform in the living room. Papaw left early for his
job near Sharpstown, and Nonny snored on in her
bedroom.

"Nonny, Shay is spending a few nights." Elva
tapped on her door. "Can you give her a ride to
work?"

"I'm not a bus service," Nonny moaned.

Elva returned to the kitchen and grabbed a
handful of powdered donuts. She loved food bank
powdered donuts.

"Nonny said no," Elva mumbled, her mouth
slightly glued shut by the thick powdery goo.

"I heard her. No prob," Shay answered from the
living room. "I'll call a friend from work to pick me

up."

Shay finished ironing, and Elva fed Bones, Christine, and M'Benga and then started her weekend yoga. Shay joined Elva on the breezeway.

"Does yoga do anything for you?" Shay asked.

"I'm extremely spry." Elva touched her forehead to her knees and then moved into warrior pose.

"I guess so," Shay said, but good-naturedly followed Elva into the pose.

A horn honked in front of the house about a half-hour into Elva's yoga session.

"That's my ride." Shay patted her ponytail and straightened her white bobby socks. "I'll see you later at Sonic."

"Later, then." Elva waved while trying to balance in lunge pose.

She tried lifting up her arms and holding onto the pose but her thoughts bounced like rubber balls, and her body wobbled like a bird on a power line. Yoga was about centering. She had to let go of her thoughts and BE, but the mysteries of plumbing kept intruding, questions about what did it mean and how she was going to do it. She cut her yoga session short with a last salutation, bowing to the sun.

She'd need deeper therapy. Time for a *Trek* fix. Elva inserted a VCR tape into the dusty machine by the TV.

Nonny exited her bedroom as the tape began to whir.

"What're you watching?"

Elva paused the tape. "It's 'Charlie X'"

"That's the one where the boy goes crazy and ends up trapped with the aliens forever," Nonny said. "I love that one."

"It's a good one." Elva agreed.

"Wait while I get a snack, and we can watch together." Nonny loved classic *Star Trek*. Elva couldn't count how many times they'd watched every episode.

Her stomach grumbled, so she followed Nonny into the kitchen. Donuts only went so far; she zapped a Hungry Man chicken nugget dinner. Nonny fixed a humongous bowl of Captain Crunch, the peanut butter kind, while Elva stopped the microwave and stirred the peas and carrots. She restarted it and casually turned over the box and read the nutrition info. Fifty-seven grams of fat. She tossed the box in the trash.

Elva joined Nonny on the couch and un-paused the tape. The theme of *Star Trek* wailed, and the Enterprise shot across the screen.

"Can I have one of your nuggets?" Nonny asked.

Elva pushed two of the greasy morsels toward her grandmother. "Take a couple."

Elva applauded herself. The move probably brought the whole meal down to less than 50 grams of fat.

She and Nonny watched and ate, slipping into a familiar pattern; one that Elva couldn't even remember beginning. Eating always meant cozying up in front of the TV under the watching eyes of

Elvis on black velvet over the couch. More than church, more than anything, Elva had been raised to have faith in two things: Elvis, the King of Rock and Roll, and *Star Trek*, the original series.

To Elva, *Star Trek* declared a future where nobody was poor. Money didn't even exist. In *Star Trek*, everybody had a shot at seeing the universe. The show demanded you do the right thing even if it hurt. It encouraged seeking out strange new worlds and boldly going. The world of *Star Trek* was a place to build on.

That's why she'd founded her fanfic group. If Loser Girls built on their own experiences, they'd be trapped forever, like poor Charlie was trapped with the aliens in this very episode. Charlie was just so messed up from his upbringing. He couldn't get away from it. Elva didn't want to be messed up like that. *Star Trek* showed another kind of world, and she was clinging to it like a life preserver.

"Oh, don't it just give you chills," Nonny said, as the episode ended with Charlie shut away with the aliens forever.

"Sure does." Elva nodded.

Nonny went back to bed, and around noon Elva fished her tennis shoes from under her dresser, and changed into a clean T-shirt. She snapped on her only pair of jeans, tucked her purple fanfic notebook in her backpack and headed down Stoke Road. The heat radiated from the blacktop road but getting Nonny up to drive her would stir up trouble. It was a two-mile walk to Belling. She'd be into town in an hour.

Sweat beaded on her face. She tried not to overly resent Nonny's depression. An empty bottle of Zoloft was gathering dust on Nonny's dresser. Since Nonny'd lost her job at Belling Elementary as a lunch lady, there'd been no health insurance. No more happy pills. They were already three months behind on the house rent. In the economic black hole of Belling, Nonny's only other job choice was to work at the chicken plant, cutting off thighs and legs. She'd have to stand up for twelve hour shifts, and her knees couldn't take it.

Elva placed her palms together and breathed in and out like a wave rushing onto the beach and back again. She had to seek positive energy. She chanted her mantra again seeking to connect herself with everything positive.

"Being poor sucks. Accepting it is the path of peace."

Today was a bookend to the day before, clear sky with a dingy yellowish haze to the east. Houston always had that dirty look. Sometimes the stench of the Gulf Coast refineries rolled in, but not today. No breeze, only humid air. The occasional screaming crow broke the silence. Half-way into town, a shiny pickup pulled around her and stopped.

"Hey there, Elva." Chase Fleaso stuck his head out the window. His rolls of chub spilled out. She'd known Chase since watching him eat his glue sticks in kindergarten.

"Hey, Chase. Why ain't you in church?"

He smelled slightly of pig, but it made sense. He *was* a nice, dependable pig farmer.

"I had to stay home and help move some stock."

Elva nodded. Chase tapped his Purina cap. The shimmering sound of cicadas surrounded them. A mocking bird chirped the calls of a dozen different birds. Elva bounced from one foot to the other on the warm blacktop and stared at him. He looked back with his mouth half-open, and his eyes sort of glazed. Chase didn't talk much. Why had he stopped? She made an attempt to fill the awkward silence.

"I'm heading to the Sonic to meet Margarett and Shay."

"I'm driving to the co-op to pick up salt licks." He slowly grinned. "You want a ride?"

He took his sweet time getting to that.

"Yeah." Elva swung off her backpack and climbed into the front seat. She tried not to gag on the overwhelming smell of pig, mixed with a dash of acrid manure.

"Shay, Margarett, and I are planning to work on our fan fiction." Elva tugged on the seatbelt.

Chase grunted. How amazingly smooth and pink his skin was. He gave the impression of a distant relative of the pig. His pimpled face sat down on pudgy globs of fat, wreathing his neck. Elva tried to imagine what sort of girl would hook up with a pig boy.

A mild jolt of alarm stabbed her when he made

a left turn away from town. Where in the heck was he going?

He gunned the engine and made another turn down the County Road Spur, a short road that led to Highway 422. Nobody turned down County Road Spur unless they planned on making out, or more, doing the deed. Elva stared at Chase in absolute horror as he pulled his truck off the road onto a flattened patch of grass.

"I'm so glad I saw you, Elva." He took off his cap. His reddish curls were plastered to his head. Chase gazed at her with soulful blue eyes. "I've been working up my nerve to get you alone for two years."

"Chase Fleaso, what are you talking about?"

Had he ever said that many words in one sentence?

He pushed back his curls, then he undid his seat belt.

"I've been in love with you since the sixth grade. I saw you there by the road and took it as a sign from God." He reached out and stroked her hair.

Elva gave Chase a good long stare. His pair of ragged Levi overalls with no shirt revealed a vast quantity of pink flesh. His Ropers were old and weathered. But was Chase a possibility? At least he was something. Chase had a secure future. She tried to imagine herself with a pig farmer, slopping pigs, showing pigs at the state fair, scrubbing pigs, shoveling manure … uh … no.

Elva yelped when his fleshy hand clamped

down on her shoulder and full blubbery lips pressed against hers. He couldn't talk fast, but he sure could move. The smell of slightly rotted catfish flooded her nostrils. She managed to not gag. She had always avoided thinking about her first kiss because she'd figured it would be exactly like this.

"Hell will freeze over before I make out with you." Elva pulled back.

"Elva, we're meant for each other." His sausage fingers waggled. She forced herself not to vomit when they grazed one boob.

She reached behind her and yanked open the truck door. She scrambled out, and Chase's rolls of fat slapped against the seat.

"I'm walking into town." Elva slammed the door shut. "Don't follow me!"

She turned tail and jogged up the road like a planet killing Doomsday machine chased after her. She flinched when she heard the squeal of Chase's truck tires peeling out and increased her speed. The bells at St. Ignatius began to ring in the distance. Dang. Dang.

Exactly.

If she didn't hurry, she'd be late meeting Margarett. She dashed through Hogg Cemetery not worrying how much bad luck was sliding her way for stepping on the graves.

She swiped her mouth in disgust. Chase Fleaso! That snake had stolen her first kiss—a catfish— breath kiss from a pig farmer.

Cece Barlow

4 FETCHING MARGARETT

Elva cut through town, passing the neat acre grounds of several churches—Aldersgate United Methodist, St. Ignatius Catholic, First Baptist, Seventh Day Adventist, and the Belling Church of Christ with its pin neat grounds. Elva used to go to the Church of Christ with Nonny every Sunday. She'd been baptized at age eight and could spit out John 3:16 without thinking. But when she turned eleven, a Sunday school teacher mouthed off at a potluck about her being born on the wrong side of the blanket. Nonny got wind of it and quit church-going permanently. Elva loved Nonny for that.

Only two churches were left in the row.

Elva cut across the lawn of the Latter Day Saints and headed into the dirt parking lot of Holiness. The building buzzed with the holy clapping, holy snapping, and holy unknown tongues (private spiritual languages only God could understand). According to Margarett, if you couldn't speak in an unknown tongue you were damned to spend eternity in Hell. How life in eternal Hell could be worse than hanging out with the tongue-talking Pentecostals for eternity baffled Elva. As she came up to the wooden steps, leading to the door, the ground vibrated from the babbling. Wild drumming rumbled within, and licks from a squealing electric guitar followed. The guitarist could sure play hot riffs.

Elva waved to Margarett, sitting on a metal folding chair by the church's front door. Margarett was beanpole thin and as pale as a vampire. Her face bones jutted at sharp angles, her elbows knobby. She wore a canary yellow jumper with a long-sleeved polyester blouse under it buttoned to her neck.

What a stupid outfit for blazing heat.

Several kids lounged on the hoods of cars in the parking lot. Enough time had passed in the service for their folks to start being slain in the spirit. The parents fell dazed to the floor, giving the Holiness kids time to sneak out and smoke cigarettes.

Elva understood the need to take the edge off.

"I've got two quarters." Margarett held out her coins. "Do you have enough so we can buy drinks at Happy Hour?"

"I've only got a dollar," Elva said. "Let's go see if we can scrounge up some more change." She couldn't bring herself to tell Margarett of the indignity of her first kiss. She spat in the dirt. Chase Fleaso, her first kiss, a fate too terrible to mention, even to one of her best friends.

"You know spitting's illegal." Margarett said. She lifted the skirt of her dress and flapped it to cool off.

Elva ignored her. "I'm sorry I'm late. Do we need to hurry?" She glanced back at Holiness. Sneaking off to the Sonic Drive-in on Sunday constituted real blasphemy for Margarett, who could be grounded or worse, switched, if caught.

"We're all right," Margarett said. "Mama and Daddy will be slain in the spirit for another couple of hours."

Elva nodded. "Then let's go scrounge for more change before we meet Shay at Sonic."

"Sounds good," Margarett said. They headed out to their favorite local parking lots and vending machines.

"Praise the Lord," Margarett squealed. She found a quarter in the Four Leaf Clover mini-mart lot.

Then Elva found another one in the Bale's Auto Body lot. That gave them an even two dollars. They passed the Alamo Ranch Bank and crossed the road to reach the Wal-Mart parking lot.

"Grandma says I have to work on Sundays," Margarett said. "I'll have to miss church."

"That'll be an adjustment," Elva said. Margarett's deli job was a heaven-sent opportunity to keep her out of that effed up church, and Elva sent a silent thank you to heaven for it. She didn't mention her plumbing job even though Shay already knew the details. Plumbing was the most exciting thing that had happened to Elva in forever. If she told Margarett now, she'd never have her moment in the sun with all three of them.

They passed Wal-Mart's automatic doors, and Elva stuck her fingers in the Coke machine change slots. Margarett checked the newspaper boxes. They peeked under the candy machines. Elva came up with a dime and Margarett with another quarter.

Elva didn't notice Chase pull up in his Chevy.

"Hey, Elva." He acted like his catfish-y breath hadn't ever snuck into her lungs.

"I'm not talking to you." Elva gave Chase a cool stare.

"Elva, don't be rude." Margarett straightened her canary jumper and smoothed her hands over her huge hair bun. She even straightened her glasses.

"Yeah, what's your problem?" Chase asked. Sweat glossed his pink skin.

"Don't you need to get back to your pigs?" Elva wished to God that Scotty could beam her up. Where was technology when she needed it?

Chase reached across the bench seat and unlocked the door. "Y'all climb in. I'll take you where you need to go."

"I'd appreciate it, Chase." Margarett pulled at the creaking handle.

"Uh, thanks," Elva said. "But no thanks." She pushed the door shut and gave Margarett a sideways glance. Her friend's eyes had a particular soulful shine. Could Margarett actually like this pig farmer? Maybe, but Elva didn't care. She was never riding with Chase again, not after that kiss.

"We're not going with you."

"Fine, be that way," Chase said. "You don't know what you'll be missing." He gunned the engine, spun his wheels, and sped out of the parking lot, causing a few random plastic bags and candy wrappers to whip in the wake.

Margarett huffed furiously. "Chase was being polite! And we could have gotten a ride!"

"I didn't know you liked Chase Fleaso." Elva raised one eyebrow.

"I don't."

"You say."

Margarett looked away from her. Elva'd never seen her so upset.

"Come on, Margarett. I'm sorry. Remember, Chase is a Baptist and thinks speaking in tongues is of the devil. It wouldn't be right to ride with him."

"That's true," Margarett answered.

"It's time to meet up with Shay. She only gets forty-five minutes for lunch. The good Lord helped us find the money we needed for our Ocean Waters. We even have enough for tax. He *wants* you to go to Sonic."

"OK, but I don't see why we couldn't take a ride from Chase. God would have forgiven us for riding with a Baptist." Margarett looked longingly in the direction that Chase's truck had gone.

5 HAPPY HOUR

Good riddance to pig boy, Elva thought as she jumped from a pile of wood pallets over a barbed wire fence into a field.

"Jump!" Elva commanded Margarett.

"My dress will tear. That ain't good stewardship."

"Come on! Pull it up and leap."

"It's not seemly!" But Margarett lifted her skirt up above her knees and jumped. Margaret wouldn't admit it, but Elva was sure these side trips to Sonic were the high point of her week even though she was flirting with the devil. Lying, soda water on Sunday … it was a slippery slope.

The girls dashed across the field land-mined with cow patties and fire ant beds. Holsteins gazed at them disinterestedly as Elva and Margarett hopped the wooden rail fence on the other side, onto the spongy blacktop of Don's parking lot. Only a few eighteen-wheelers were parked in the lot. It would be packed at suppertime. Elva loved Don's slabs of greasy chicken-fried steak and mounds of real mashed potatoes. She especially loved the thick gravy flecked with peppercorns and on the side, crispy, buttery Texas toast.

She pitied Margarett. Her friend had never had one of those delicious meals. Don's had a bar and a pool table, and Margarett's parents saw it as the fiery gates of Hell, the first step of damning iniquity. Elva had no words for the effed-up-ness of that.

Providentially, Shay waited outside the restaurant, so Margarett wouldn't be tempted to step inside. In the shadows, Elva eyed a thin guy dressed in Wranglers and a faded cowboy shirt. Something about his body language sent an uncomfortable shiver up Elva's spine. Shay spoke to the lurking guy. He flicked a cigarette into a trashcan by the door and went back into the restaurant. Shay jogged toward them.

"Who's the old guy?" Elva asked.

"That's Bobby Ray, and he's only twenty-five. He takes in the gas money." Shay flipped her ponytail and smoothed out her short candy-striped skirt. "What took y'all so long?"

"We'd have been here faster, but Elva refused to take a ride from Chase Fleaso," Margarett said.

"Why ever not?" Shay asked.

Elva didn't answer. A flush of heat rushed into her face.

"What are you not telling us?" Shay asked.

"She thought it was unseemly to ride with a Baptist," Margarett said.

"You've never cared if anyone was Baptist or not." Shay gave Elva a sharp look.

"Let's hustle over to Sonic," Elva said. "I need help with my new story. I'm trying to decide what kind of boyfriend T'Pak should have."

"Who's T'Pak again?" Margarett asked.

Elva's instant plan to change the subject was working.

"Spock's long lost daughter," Elva said.

"You know Spock's love child," Shay said. "From when he had that affair with the Betazed on planet Risa. The woman was one of Troi's ancestors. But I want to hear more about Chase."

"Nothing is going on with Chase," Elva said, wincing because she'd protested way too much. Margarett was clueless, but Shay, Shay knew Elva was hiding something, but she could talk about it yet. The Chase Incident had rubbed her too raw.

They sprinted across the blistering pavement to the Sonic.

She and Margarett were out of breath when they plopped down at the picnic table under the red awning in front of the Sonic Drive-in. Margarett pushed the call button on the square metal intercom. Elva leaned forward and spoke. "We'd like three extra large Ocean Waters."

Nothing cooled like an icy Ocean Water. The taste of Sprite tinted blue and blasted with coconut-goodness syrup was their favorite. Best of all, every single drink was priced half-off in the afternoon.

"Make that one Ocean Water with double ice, please." Shay interrupted, and then she smiled at Elva and Margarett. "I'm trying to lose weight."

Elva ignored that statement. Shay wore a juniors' size 12 and what was the problem with that? Elva reached in her pocket and pulled out four quarters and two dimes. Margarett put out her dollar and change, but Shay waved her hand.

"This is my treat," she said. "I've already made $42 in tips today.

Neither Margarett nor Elva peeped an argument. Shay was a millionaire. They gratefully tucked their money back in their pockets.

"Thanks," Margarett said.

"Don't give it a thought," Shay replied.

"I won't," Elva said and laughed.

"Elva, you ought to be more thankful to the Lord," Margarett said.

Shay laughed. "If you get all religious on me, Elva Presley Hicks, I'll never pay for another drink at Sonic, not ever. One holy-roller in our group is enough."

Margarett sniffed. "Faith is the most important thing in the world."

"Don't argue, gals," Elva begged. "This might be our last day together for over a week."

A waitress skated up to their table with three

large Styrofoam cups. She thunked them down.

"The one with the mark on top has the extra ice." The waitress popped her gum bubble, and Shay handed her a five.

"Keep the change," Shay said.

Margarett reached for one of the cups. "God bless you for buying."

"If I believed in God." Shay ripped paper off her straw and squished it into her drink.

"I have an important announcement to make," Elva said, after a brain-numbing swallow of her coconutty-sweet Ocean Water.

"Your grandpa says you can work at Don's?" Shay jumped in, not waiting for Elva to explain. "I just love my job. And Bobby Ray, he's no boy, mind you, he's a man. He wants to take me out. And there's more, we get in a real live band on Friday nights, the one that plays over at the VFW Hall sometimes."

Elva tapped the tabletop to bring the meeting of the Loser Girls to order, but Margarett cut in again.

"I sure would like to go to the VFW Hall and try dancing." Margarett stared down at her anklet socks and sandals. "But I know it's a sin."

Dang, that did it. Job news and fanfic would have to wait. Margarett had said a shockingly normal thing, and it couldn't be ignored. She had to be encouraged to be normal, and not many opportunities presented themselves.

"What did you say? You want go dancing?" Elva slapped the table. "Everything in the universe is stopping right now."

"I almost believe in God." Shay put in.

"Shay, take off Saturday night and rustle up dates," Elva said. "We're going dancing. We have to."

"It's a pact!" Shay placed her hand over Elva's.

"C'mon, Margarett." Elva nudged Margarett with her shoulder, and with a trembling hand Margarett placed her hand on top.

Elva made it her business to guide the Loser Girls. Who else would make sure Margarett had a life? Not her crazy tongue-spouting parents. And not that snake, Brother Lavine. Dear God, the holy-rolling Pentecostals were hardly better than the polygamist Mormons. They'd already effed up Margarett's life enough. She was just one inch from being pregnant with a 50-year-old husband.

"But I don't know how to dance." Margarett drew her hand back and her lower lip trembled. "And I might go to Hell." Tears welled in her eyes.

"Oh, Margarett, God don't send people to hell for dancing." Elva shook her head, torn between laughing and crying. The thing about the Loser Girls, they came to one another's rescue. They watched each others' backs. They were family.

"Even a sinner like me knows that dancing's okay," Shay said.

"It's settled. We're going two-stepping next Saturday night," Elva said.

Margarett had a bemused expression on her face, like the Holy Ghost had settled on her like a dove. Shay would find her a date, and Margarett was going dancing. Amen.

"So Elva, when are you starting work at Don's?" Shay asked and finally the conversation swung back Elva's way.

Elva shook her head. "Nope, I'm not. I told you that."

"You aren't really planning to plumb, are you?" Shay asked. "I thought for sure you'd ditch it and work at Don's." She sprinkled salt on her wrist and licked it. She followed it with a huge swig of Ocean Water.

"Papaw got me a job with Carus Residential and Industrial." Elva took another long sip of her blue concoction and fixed her eyes on the awning overhead.

Poor Margarett was so overcome by that statement that her mouth hung open, and a dribble of blue ran down her chin. "You can't do man's work." She swiped it away.

"Do you really want to work for a plumbing company?" Shay asked. "I know you said so last night, but you can still change your mind."

"I'm not." Elva sucked up more of her drink.

"You can't do it." Margarett cut in. "It's unseemly."

"What kind of word is unseemly?" Elva asked.

"A gal plumbing, it's dishonoring God." Margarett tweaked her bun. "Shirtless, wild, cursing men and all."

"Hush with the Pentecostal nonsense," Shay

said. "This is the new millennium."

"I'm getting $17.13 an hour," Elva said, "And I hope to God I'll catch a shirtless, wild, cursing man."

Silence. Had the $17.13 shut up Margarett or was it the thought of a shirtless, wild, cursing man?

"Now, that must be the Holy Ghost working." Shay laughed. Her ponytail bobbed left and right.

"I can't argue the money," Margarett finally said, slurping the last taste of her Ocean Water. "I can't argue it at all. What a blessing!" She didn't mention the shirtless, wild, cursing man but she didn't argue him either.

"When do you start?" Shay asked.

"Tomorrow," Elva said. "I'm heading to the Wal-Mart Supercenter tonight to buy a pair of steel-toed boots for my job."

"Umm, interesting." Shay struggled to put on a weak smile.

Margarett tucked a loose bobby pin into her bun. "Do you have to wear pants?"

Elva looked at Margarett crossways. "Every single day, thank God!"

"At least you're keeping your eyes on the Lord," Margarett said. "Thanking God like that."

They burst out laughing.

"I will thank God every day, Margarett, and double on payday." Elva crossed her heart.

"So tell me more about this T'Pak," Margarett said.

"I've got some notes." Shay patted her pockets.

Elva placed the hardcopy of their story on the table. She wished for a laptop to enter the changes directly. The first thing she planned to buy with plumbing cash was a Mac.

"Here's my idea, adding an intense flirting scene with Kirk and T'Pak's friend Tré might spice up our story." Shay spread out a folded sheet covered with scribbled writing.

Elva scanned the page. "I think we could work this in after the Gorn puberty rite."

"I'm not sure if that's realistic. Tré is only sixteen and Kirk is like a hundred." Margarett said. "Maybe adding something in about a girl who works as a butcher would be better."

Margarett was trekking more than usual. *Yay!*

"We could call her Brigitte, and she could chop up meat for the ugly lizard people," Shay said. "And I think Tré likes older men."

"The Gorn, not lizard people." Elva corrected. "I like the idea of the Brigitte character. She could be somebody else's long-lost daughter, too, perhaps Dr. McCoy's." Elva leaned enthusiastically over the pages. "Margarett's got a good point about Tré and Kirk too. It's just too creepy."

They spent the next minutes working furiously and munching tasty morsels of Ocean Water ice. Elva's hand was cramping when Shay jumped up.

"Look at the time! I've got to get back to Don's. I'm late." Shay whipped out a comb and smoothed her ponytail. "Are we meeting next week?"

"Same place, same time?" Margarett asked.

"Absolutely," Elva said.

"I'll see y'all here next Sunday," Shay yelled back, as she ran back across the highway to Don's.

"I better get back to Holiness," Margarett said. "Mama and Daddy are probably coming out from under the Spirit. I'm supposed to serve at the potluck at Brother Lavine's house. Do you want to come?"

"Uh, I'll pass this time," Elva said.

No social desperation would ever entice her to visit Brother Lavine's house. She downed the last crunchy bits of ice in her cup and would have headed straight home, but she decided to make a detour through Hogg Cemetery. The Universe was already pissed off at her, and she'd run over some graves after Chase's kiss. She picked a handful of yellow cornflowers from the ditch and reverently began dropping a yellow flower on each grave as a peace offering.

Disrespecting the dead might mess with her karma. She might be cursed to live in Belling her whole life. She didn't have a parent's couch to sit on for the rest of her days. Nonny and Papaw were getting up there. She had to get a life going.

Elva dropped another flower.

6 STEEL-TOED BOOTS

Later, Elva asked Papaw to take her to the library. Nonny was snoozing away, so Papaw and Elva headed to town alone. He dropped her off at the door.

"I'll be over to Billy's Ice House for an hour," he said.

Elva nodded, "Have fun." She smiled as she pulled open the library's grimy glass door. She had one glorious hour to surf the net and peruse her favorite sites before the library closed. She rushed through the inner doors and looked across the computers in dismay. Every station was being used.

"I thought you might come by." The librarian, Mrs. Cook, waved at Elva from behind her desk. "I reserved the computer in the carrel for you."

"Oh thank you, Mrs. Cook! Thank you." Elva couldn't help a few excited hops.

Mrs. Cook adjusted her silver pointy glasses. "You're welcome, dear."

Elva hurried to the carrel. She typed in her library card number three times before she got it right, trying not to be overwhelmed by excitement. She clicked the mouse and surfed to her blog. Offering tantalizing glimpses of her current fanfic kept her readers interested, and she hadn't posted anything in two weeks.

She copied her blog entry from her flash drive to all her feeds. It only took a minute to delete the spam, and then check her blog stats. Yay, two more real hits! People were out there quivering in anticipation for her big Internet splashdown.

She surfed over to her favorite fanfic forums to check out the current competition. Her worst story was excessively better than anything posted there. She crafted a couple of thoughtful critique comments for the better fanfic attempts, and then hurried over to her favorite GAFF (GodAwful FanFic Forum), to read the hysterical stuff, especially the one about the Enterprise visiting the Pentecostal planet.

The computer beeped.

Five more minutes! It seemed like she'd only been online for moments. She jumped over to one last serious forum and scanned quickly. It was all crap there, too.

Dang, the blue screen of death popped up. Her

computer time had ended.

As she exited the library, Elva waved at Mrs. Cook. Papaw waited in the parking lot. They headed over to the Wal-Mart Supercenter to buy her plumbing clothes. Her dive into plumbing brought to mind some sort of space anomaly that led who knows where. Excited butterflies and queasy sickness flooded her stomach at the same time. New clothes weren't something Elva got often. She let a ray of pleasure shine into her heart even if they were plumbing clothes. She always said she didn't like shopping, she liked buying.

"Wal-Mart's got the best prices on steel-toed boots," Papaw said. "You'll need thick socks, some Dickies, and a pack of t-shirts."

At least her clothes would be new. Papaw settled down in the snack bar with a Coke while Elva trailed up the narrow shoe aisles with a cart.

When her shopping was finished, Elva got Papaw and they joined the checkout line. They purchased one pair of monster-sized tan boots, a pack of thick gray socks, a package of red t-shirts, and two pairs of tan Dickies overalls with a soil release finish.

The total?

Over a hundred dollars. A staggering sum. More than she had spent on all her school clothes the previous year. She paid no mind to the pinprick in her heart of having so much less than many girls her age. That unfortunate state was about to change, and she was in charge of the changing. The thought energized her so much so, she convinced Papaw to fill Nonny's Zoloft prescription.

Nonny was still asleep when they got home. Elva put the Zoloft on the kitchen counter and wrote a note.

Hope this helps, Love, Elva Presley

She fed Bones, Christine, and M'Benga, stroking their tiny hooves. After, she took a cool shower and laid her clothes over a chair in her room.

"We're leaving early," Papaw said. "Jump in bed now."

It was almost nine.

"I'll just finish this scene in my story, and then it's lights out."

"Don't tell me tomorrow that I didn't warn you," Papaw said.

"I heard you," Elva said. "I'll be ready."

At ten, Shay tapped on Elva's bedroom window. Elva pushed it open

"How was work?" she asked as Shay navigated her way inside, dragging a bulging plastic garbage bag behind her. Elva had no clue how long Shay would stay. A week? A month? Shay's stays varied, depending on how long it took her mama to figure out that her boyfriend of the month was another ultimate loser.

"I only made $30 in tips after lunch." Shay rolled off the bed and dusted at a black smudge on her white Keds. "Heck, I got my shoes dirty."

"It'll come out," Elva said. "Are you hungry? I think there're leftovers in the fridge."

"Bobby Ray bought me a hamburger with fries during my break."

"Bobby Ray?" Elva asked. "Isn't he that old guy?"

"He's only twenty-five, remember?"

"Uh, you're sixteen," Elva said.

"Age don't mean nothing," Shay said, pulling off her shoes and socks and reaching for her robe in the bag.

"In Texas, it's called statutory rape." Elva shot back.

"Bobby Ray just bought me a hamburger, Elva." Shay shook her head. "You don't know anything about anything."

Elva didn't answer. She didn't know anything about anything. She'd had one fishy kiss. A real man bought Shay a hamburger. That was Experience.

"You want to read my new fanfic pages?" Elva asked.

Shay laughed and said, "Maybe later," and headed to the shower. Elva kept writing. Her words flew across the page. T'Pak, seventeen in Vulcan years, wanted to date a hot 25-year-old technician, a perfectly legal act, but T'Pak's best friend, Tré, underage at sixteen, dated an Andorian illegally.

T'Pak moved down the hallway to a barred cell. Bruised but unharmed, Tré cowered in a corner.

"Why didn't you learn your lesson with Admiral Kirk?" T'Pak asked. "Older men are trouble. You should

be glad that the Andorians merely threw you in prison. Your Andorian lover was executed an hour ago. His crime? Making out with an alien underage girl."

Tré screamed, "No!"

Her agonized cries reverberated against the walls of the cell.

Elva could feel the agony in her character, clutching at her throat. She'd put reality on the page. More words flew. One page, two, three pages. A half-hour later Elva was still on a roll, but she stopped. She went to get Shay to look at the pages, but she was conked out on the couch. Elva powered down her computer and climbed into bed. She set her alarm so she'd have time for goat care.

What would tomorrow hold?

***

Buzzzz. Buzzzz. Buzzzz.

Hell.

Elva moaned as she swung her feet onto the floor. What time had she set the alarm for? She rubbed her eyes, focusing on the red numbers on the clock: 4:00 A.M.

God help her.

She focused on her breath. In. Out. Whatever plumbing could toss at her, she'd face it head on. Her Loser Girl lifetime had worked in grit. She'd plumb.

Heck, yeah, she would.

She tossed off her sleeping shirt and shorts and snapped on her worn, sagging bra. She pulled on the soft t-shirt and stepped into the stiff Dickies overalls. Elva checked out her new outfit in the mirror. The Dickies certainly had a permanent crease up the front of the legs. Her bare toes graced with purple luster polish peeked out from the tan cloth.

She turned for the side view. The overalls were tight around the hips, but loose at the waist, leaving a big gap. She shrugged. It couldn't be helped. Elva picked up her boots and socks and headed toward the kitchen. She had to feed the kids. She'd never let them down.

In the living room, Shay opened an eye as Elva passed and mumbled, "Mama, get your own beer."

"Go back to sleep," Elva whispered.

Shay complied by pulling a pillow over her head. Elva sat at the kitchen table and put on her thick socks and laced her boots. Her feet felt like they were encased in concrete.

Next, she put on the water to boil for the kids' formula. Papaw's razor hummed in the bathroom. Nonny snored in her bedroom like a buzz saw. Elva set up the Coke bottles for the kids' bottles but poured off some hot water into a cup. She added a package of hot chocolate mix and filled the bottles while stirring her drink.

Outside the breezeway window in the pitch black sky, Elva could see the swath of the Milky Way. An owl hooted in the distance. Bones, Nurse

Chapel, and M'Benga were definitely not used to this early hour and snoozed on a weathered blue towel. She sipped the chocolate, enjoying the sugar rush.

She hated to wake them but had no choice. She picked up Bones and tucked him under her arm. His tummy was flat as a pancake. He rolled his head and wiggled joyfully. The Universe had threaded joy into every wiggle of a baby goat. She tried to offer him the bottle but he kept butting and not latching onto the nipple.

"Maa."

His cute voice tickled her insides, and she gave him a cuddly hug. Bones finally began sucking the bottle. She dozed off until the familiar vacuum sound of an empty bottle roused her enough to put Bones down. She picked up Nurse Chapel, smoothing a hand over the baby's sleek coat. She began the feeding process again. After came M'Benga. Her eyes drifted shut again before his bottle emptied.

"Gal, didn't you hear me calling." Papaw stood at the door.

Elva stifled a yawn. "I've got to refill the bottles for Nonny and then I'll come." She shook her head to clear the warm fuzzies.

"Let Nonny take care of the dang goats. We've gotta go."

"She won't do it," Elva said.

"She's got her dang pills," Papaw answered.

"Those won't kick in for at least a week." Elva

gathered the milk bottles. "She won't be worth anything until then."

"Just leave 'em," Papaw growled.

"I can't. These goats are worth some money."

That shut up Papaw. He didn't have the capacity to understand her knack for goat care. Money he could understand.

"Meet me in the truck when you're finished," Papaw grumbled.

Elva made more bottles for Nonny and put them in the fridge. Papaw waited in his plumbing truck.

"Get in," he said. "I don't want to be late."

Elva opened the door and stared at the piles. Tools littered the floorboard and the seat was covered with stacks of plans, coffee cups, Coke cans, and fittings. She wanted to cry that plumbing was way too much for her.

But she had to do this.

"Just shove it all over." Papaw turned on the engine.

Elva thrust over as much of the junk as she could and plopped her behind on top of the rest. That was that, she was on her way to plumb.

7 THE SHOP

As they moved into the thick suburbs of Houston, Papaw turned off the highway into a Whataburger parking lot. The orange and white awning was muted in the early morning gray.

"How about breakfast?" he asked.

"Sounds good," Elva said.

Papaw pulled up to the drive through speaker.

"Order what you want," he said. "You've got a big day in front of you."

Elva didn't have to think. "I'd like a large Coke, fries, and a double-meat Whataburger with cheese and jalapenos."

The foil-wrapped hamburger came steaming hot. She bit into the juicy meat with the bite of peppers. Gooey American cheese and mustard oozed from the edges of the fluffy white bun. The fries were crispy outside and melty inside, the Coke extra fizzy.

Elva munched the last fry as they entered the plumbing shop parking lot. She licked her fingers. A man in his twenties straddled a gold Harley outside the dull metal shop building.

He wore a Stetson, but it didn't hide his chiseled face—a *GQ* God, sculpted, perfect. Elva climbed out of the truck, and he gave *her* "the look," the honest to God "checking you out" look.

Let him look, she thought. Her double D boobs weren't one of the most common sights in the universe.

A very short man, even shorter than Papaw, scurried out of a corrugated metal garage door.

"Get your damn butts to your damn jobs on time, damn it. I damn sure don't want to lose any more damn money. Damn it all to hell."

Everyone nodded, so Elva obliged by nodding too.

"Mr. Bob, what about my gal?" Papaw asked.

"Elva Presley?" One man snickered and 'damn' man, Mr. Bob, laughed out loud.

"Damn, I didn't think your damn granddaughter would show, damn it." He put his hand on his head and shouted with laughter.

Elva tried to smile but instead stretched her lips over her teeth like a Rottweiler rubbed the wrong way. What had she thought it would be like?

"The gal gets one damn week trial. Elva's assigned to Yves's damn team today," Mr. Bob said.

"At the damn valve company."

"Should we start Elva out on industrial?" Papaw asked.

"You said she could do the damn work."

"She can, but, hell, it's an industrial job."

"I can do it." Elva stepped forward. "Who's Yves?" She surveyed the group of men standing in a semi-circle.

"I'm Yves." Another short man answered. He was maybe thirty with thinning hair and hazel eyes. Elva stuck her hand out, and he stared at her with a half-opened mouth. Not a good first contact situation, but he finally took her offered hand.

The *GQ* God stepped up and smiled at her. "I'm Wyatt." His fingers wrapped around her hand. Warmth shot up from her stomach to her face like water bursting from an artesian well.

"You look pretty sturdy." Wyatt leaned toward her, smiling. How did he get his teeth that white? He smelled forestry-like and clean, and she couldn't help taking a deep whiff.

"I'm Elva." Her face turned hot.

"Pleased to meet you." Wyatt doffed his hat and placed it over his heart.

Elva ducked her head. "Likewise."

"We're with Yves. Follow me." He headed to a nearby plumbing truck.

Elva paid particular attention to his backside. Wyatt had bulging muscles and skin-tight Levi's.

They all climbed in the pick-up and sped away from the shop, taking side streets. Yves was driving, and Wyatt had pulled his hat over his eyes. Elva sat in the middle, smashed up against Wyatt's leg. She wished for a cell phone so she could contact Shay and Margarett and covertly describe every delicious Wyatt detail.

"Here's the supply house." Yves broke the silence. He pulled into a crowded narrow parking lot. A sign hung over the door of the corrugated metal building: Moore Plumbing Supply. Twenty trucks from various plumbing outfits were lined up. Elva readied herself for beaming down to a new planet. She smoothed her hair and wished she'd brought a scrunchie.

"Wyatt, go around back and pull 16 joints of CPVC pipe for the pressure application." Yves said as he climbed out the truck.

Where was a universal translator when you needed one?

Wyatt nodded and set off around the building.

"Come on, Hicks," Yves said. "The boys will have the rest of my order ready inside."

Elva hopped out of the truck and followed Yves into the plumbing supply. Inside, an air conditioner blew full blast, plunging the room into arctic conditions.

"Did you get my order?" Yves asked man at the counter.

"We did." The man was big, real big, like a walrus.

"Who's the little lady?" he asked.

Elva glanced around for the lady.

"Hicks? She's on the Carus's payroll." Yves said.

She glanced again at the man at the counter. He licked his globular lips like Elva was a morsel of fried chicken.

"Elva, carry my order out to the truck," Yves said. "Those boxes, there, on the floor."

Elva picked up a large box of fittings and backed out the door. The parking lot had emptied. Their truck was loaded with pipe on the topside rack. The truck bed was a mess of tools, fittings, and trash. Had the plumbers ever heard of the word organize? Where was she supposed to wedge in this box? She shoved over a tangle of cords and several cans of Pistol Pete glue and dropped the box into the resulting open space. She went back for the other box. It weighed a ton.

Walrus man and Yves laughed as she tried to lift it. After her third attempt, someone stepped beside her.

"If you can't lift the whole box, empty out half of it." The voice was gravelly, and Elva didn't recognize it.

She muttered, not looking up, "Thanks."

She skittered in surprise when a heavy box landed next to hers. A pair of deeply tanned hands with neatly clipped fingernails reached to help her unload the cans, but as she stood, her head connected with the mystery helper's head in a resounding crack.

"Ouch." Elva sat back on her haunches and rubbed the spot.

A boy about her age, tomato stake thin, and way over six feet tall, smiled at her. "You can say that again." The deep timbre of the guy's voice sent a tingly quiver down her spine. His shoulder length brown hair was smooshed around his head and his creamy Catalina cowboy hat rested upside down beside his boots. "Are you alright?"

This new boy was a hottie, but not quite a GQ god. His face was all planes, harsh, angled. She touched the base of her throat at her vocal chords. No sound came.

"Do you want help?" he asked, gently shaking her shoulder.

Elva shook her head. "Naw, I'm good."

She struggled to lift the half-empty box, managing to rest it on her hip.

The boy laughed, and the sound rumbled in her chest.

"Independent streak. I like that." He tapped on his hat.

"She's a firecracker." Walrus man laughed.

The boy headed out the door without a word, no name, nothing. She gave his tight backside an appraising glance. *Nice.*

"Hicks, get a move on," Yves said, slurping coffee.

"Done." She hurried to dump the cans in the truck and return for the rest. Wyatt was up topside, securing even more pipe to the rack as she finished.

"Is that the last of it?" Wyatt asked.

"Yep." Elva said.

Yves exited the plumbing supply. "Let's go. Pile in the truck."

Elva climbed in without a word. Wyatt followed her.

"Hicks, did you put both the boxes in the back?" Yves asked.

Her whole right side pressed up against Wyatt. She was about to pass out from the sensory overload.

"I did," Elva said and kept breathing.

Yves peeled out of the parking lot and shot down the road.

Wyatt tensed up next to her. A muscle twitched in his cheek, like he wanted to say something. Yves gunned the engine and turned onto a side street. She yelped as they bounced over some railroad tracks. She bit her tongue. The salty taste of blood flooded her mouth. Elva heard sickening thunks, cracks, and ker-crunches outside the truck.

"Hell!" Yves pulled over. "Hicks, did you tie down the damn boxes?"

She froze. Was she supposed to tie down the 'damn boxes?'

"Go see what you can salvage," Yves said.

"I'll help her pick up the mess." Wyatt offered.

"Hell, no," Yves said. "Hicks needs to clean up her own damn messes. I told Mr. Bob this wouldn't work."

Elva squared her chin, and, hell, no, she wasn't going to cry. Not one stupid tear.

"Don't take all day picking up this crap!" Yves thumped the dashboard with his fist.

8 PLUMBING

Elva looked in dismay at the scattered fittings. Several had shattered into pieces. She gathered up the ones on the road first, jumping out of the way of two speeding cars. Next, she picked her way into the briar bushes that filled the ditch for the rest.

"I see that look on your face, Elva Presley Hicks." Wyatt had followed her. "Quitting is a bad idea. Yves'll leave you here with no way home, and this isn't a particularly safe part of town." Wyatt's voice was soothing; his deep blue eyes, friendly.

"Are you through yet?" Yves screamed from the pickup.

Elva nodded slightly at Wyatt, handing her box up the embankment. He made a good point. She'd quit tomorrow.

"They don't grow them too smart in podunk

Texas." Yves charged out of the truck. He grabbed the box from her and hefted it into the back. "Tie the damn things down this time."

Wyatt handed her a tie-down. She stretched it over the box and was about to attach it when the thick rubber tie-down snapped and hit her square in the face.

Yves laughed. "That serves you right. "

She willed herself not to yelp in pain. God, it hurt. She glanced over at Wyatt. A flicker of admiration lurked in his eyes. A glimpse of her live long and prosper spirit had bubbled out, and, miracle, Wyatt had seen it. She reached for the tie-down again and hooked it securely.

"Let's get going," Yves said.

Elva stumbled as she climbed in the truck. Her face really hurt. How could she last six more hours?

Yves raced down a labyrinth of streets until he finally took a feeder street, heading onto the freeway. Wyatt pulled his Stetson over his eyes and leaned against the window.

"Damn." Yves hit the steering wheel. Elva gazed at the unending line of vehicles. The freeway looked like a parking lot. "This'll set us back another hour, maybe two." Yves flipped the radio to the screeching sounds of heavy metal. He took a short brown cigarette out of the ashtray and lit it, taking a deep draw. One whiff revealed the same smell that lurked behind the gym at Belling High. At least the feeling of hunger had been chased away. Pot had a way of doing that to her.

And she'd thought Belling High School was hell.

Elva was oozy-goozy from pot by the time they reached the jobsite.

"Time for work." Yves's words were slurred, and his eyes were glazed.

Elva almost fell when she got out and was grateful for Wyatt's steadying hand.

She peered through the two wide double doors of the jobsite—the building was big enough to put a good sized airplane in it. The floor inside was dirt with rebar. "What do they do here anyway?"

"This is a valve manufacturing plant," Wyatt said. "They make valves for corrosive industrial applications."

Tech, tech, tech. Surprisingly, plumbing and warp drives had similar convoluted technical descriptions.

Wyatt tapped on a white hard hat. "White hats are for journeymen. You're yellow."

"So what does yellow mean?" Elva asked, snapping on the hat's strap.

"Helper/Go-for," Wyatt said.

They crossed the huge warehouse. Hulking pieces of machinery hummed. Wyatt left her at a roughed-in door on the far wall.

"Carry those jugs to the water station by the big door," he said and left her to the task.

"$17.13. $17.13," Elva muttered after she filled a jug and trekked to the water station with it. "Every hour, $17.13."

Numbers were as sacred as words. She dropped the jug by the water station table and sank down to the floor. Wyatt came behind her. "Sitting on the job will get you fired."

Yves walked up. "Wyatt, have you finished that pressure test?"

"I'm getting Elva on task," Wyatt said.

"Leave Hicks to me."

Wyatt shrugged and headed toward some scaffolding.

"You better hustle or I'll see your butt fired," Yves barked. "Do you understand me?"

"Yes, sir!" She hopped to her feet and would have saluted if she'd had a free hand.

Moving the jugs made her feel like she was running a marathon in the Olympics. Sweat stung her eyes, and her joints creaked from exertion.

"At least you got the job done." Yves seemed to come out of nowhere when she put down the last jug. "Time for real work. You're my go-for, and tomorrow come with a damn tool belt or don't come back."

Elva stumbled after him.

Yves stopped a few feet past her. "Crap, move."

And that's what she did. Elva moved into a solid rhythm, fetching each thing Yves asked for with minimal conversation.

She spent the whole day hauling a never-ending stream of tools, fittings, and pipe.

9 CHEF BOYARDEE

After work, Elva waited for Papaw at the shop. Wyatt took off on his motorcycle, and Yves left in his truck. She sank down beside a light pole in the humid heat and rested her eyes. She'd put in ten hours in one day. That was almost two hundred in take home pay. It occurred to her that she could afford a pair of Sevens from an upscale store. No way could she quit.

The sky had turned a faded purple, and bats circled above the street lamp when Papaw picked her up.

"What happened to your eye?" he asked, reaching across the cab and unlocking the door.

Elva swung the side mirror toward her face. A thick half-ring of black had formed under it. She gently touched the puffy skin. Yves and Wyatt hadn't mentioned her black eye once.

"A tie-down snapped me in the face."

"It don't look too bad," Papaw said.

"I guess not." Elva shrugged. "Yves says I need a tool belt with basic stuff—gloves, a level, hammer, tape measure, pliers."

Papaw grunted. "A real plumber would provide a tool belt for his helper."

Elva climbed into the truck. "He said don't come back without one." Waves of tiredness closed over her. Her eyes drifted shut as they left the parking lot.

The next thing she knew Papaw was shaking her shoulder.

"We're home," he said.

A loaded tool belt rested on the seat next to her. "I stopped for the belt at Lowe's. I didn't have the heart to wake you."

Elva squeezed Papaw's hand and stumbled into the house. A sweet tomato smell wafted toward her. Eight dripping cans of Chef Boyardee Spaghetti Os were piled in the sink. A pot of slimy Os dotted with oozy meatballs simmered on the stove.

"Are y'all ready for dinner?" Nonny asked from the recliner in the living room.

Elva spooned the Os over a smiling Elvis face in the bowl's bottom. Nonny entered the kitchen with a shriek.

"What happened to you, Elva Presley?" Nonny asked. Her mouth gaped open like a river gar left to die on the bank.

"She got banged up at work," Papaw said. Elva noted a lilt in his voice that curled up like smoke flowing from a cigarette butt.

"A tie-down snapped me in the face," Elva said, forking up sauce drenched Os and meatballs. Heaven.

"Would you like an aspirin?" Nonny asked. Her belief in aspirin rivaled any Holy Ghost faith healing.

"I'm good." Elva shoved another spoonful of Spaghetti Os into the corner of her mouth and gloried in the flavor of Chef Boyardee. In the middle of her next bite, she heard a pitiful wail from the goats.

"Nonny, did you feed the kids today?" Elva asked.

"I fed them." Nonny answered, but didn't meet Elva's eyes. "I went out at lunchtime and gave them the bottles you fixed."

"Did you feed them in the late afternoon?"

"I was puny then," Nonny said.

More like she couldn't pull herself away from her soaps. Elva reached for a saucepan to heat some water for the formula. Was there a Soap Opera Anonymous for people with this mind-numbing addiction?

While she poured the goats' bottles, the phone rang. Elva shoved the receiver between her chin and shoulder.

"I'm on break." Shay said. "I wanted to know how your first plumbing day went."

"I'm here too." Margarett jumped right in over Shay. "Our phone's back on, praise the Lord!"

A three-way call! Elva almost dropped the bottle and the phone. Maybe they'd get in some fanfic time.

"Today was okay for me too. I fetched stuff, and omigod the cutest guy works with me. His name is Wyatt. The only bad thing—I got a freaking black eye."

"Sorry. A frozen vegetable bag might help." Shay offered.

"I learned how to use the luncheon meat slicer today," Margaret cut in. "And Chase Fleaso came by two times. First, he bought a pound of bologna, and then he brought me a bottle of cherry Pepsi. He's so nice." She was never this chatty.

"I'm glad you think so." Shay cut in. "Because he's the boy taking you dancing on Saturday."

"What!" Margarett and Elva spoke at the same time, but Elva's voice pitched way higher.

"Keep your voice down, Elva," Margarett whispered and then said with muffled words, "Mama, I ain't doing nothing untoward. Elva is excited about her new job. Don't make me hang up."

"Margarett, be calm and everything will be all right," Elva said. "Tell your mama we're talking the Bible."

"Nothing is going on, Mama." Margarett's voice

wobbled. "In the name of Jesus, I promise."

"Are you OK?" Elva asked Margarett. Her mama didn't spare the rod.

"Yeah, Mama's gone into the kitchen," Margarett whispered. "She's frying chicken so I can still talk."

"Elva, why are you so freaked out about Chase Fleaso?" Shay didn't wait for an answer. "Are you jealous of Chase? I didn't think you liked him."

"I don't!"

"Well, it sounds like you do."

"Mama, I'm coming," Margarett called. "I've got to go. I can't wait for Saturday night. I probably won't be in touch with y'all until then." Her phone clicked off.

"So what's the deal about Chase?" Shay asked.

Elva had to cut off this Chase interrogation.

"I can't stand Chase," Elva said. "He's a pig farmer, and I've got standards."

"OK, OK." Shay laughed. "I believe you. Now for your news, be ready with your dancing shoes on Saturday too. You've got a date."

"What! Who is he? Oh no, what about my black eye?" Elva touched the puffy spot and winced.

"Concealer," Shay said impatiently. "It's make-up. I have some if you don't have any. Our skin tones are sort of similar."

"So who's the guy anyway?" Elva asked.

"Oops, my break is over." Shay ended the call.

"Talk to you later," Elva said anyway.

She had a date! *Yay!*

Elva hung up the phone and whistled while finishing the bottles.

Later, Elva tried to focus on her fanfic while feeding the goats. She mapped out the next scenes of their story: T'Pak could go to a dance with her friends Tré and Brigitte. It could be a blind date. Elva tried to imagine what sort of hot Starfleet officers might be a good fit for T'Pak. Maybe a sizzling American Indian or a cute Scottish hottie? Would they get past first base? Do the deed? Would he be a science officer or command staff? She picked up another goat. Command, definitely command.

The busyness of the day had caught up with her. She yawned. Her eyelids sank downward.

"Elva, wake up, wake up." It was Shay, home from work.

Elva stretched her cramped legs and arms. A warm goat cuddled next to her belly.

"What time is it?"

"I'd say almost midnight." Shay sat next to Elva on the steps. "Oooh, that eye looks worse than you said."

Elva tucked Bones next to Christine and M'Benga.

"It don't hurt." Elva yawned.

"Are you sure you don't want to work at Don's?" Shay untied her Keds.

"No, and I don't want to talk about it." Elva kissed each velvety goat nose and headed in the house. "You take the bed, and I'll take the couch tonight."

Elva lay flat on her back on the couch and relaxed the muscles in her face, then her arms, and legs, and body. She connected each calming movement to her breath. She leaned back her neck and arched her spine, opening up her heart.

As she drifted off, she realized she hadn't written one word of her fanfic story.

Not one dang word.

10 VFW HALL DANCE

The next few days, Elva served as Wyatt's go-for. The grueling work sapped the life out of her. Every night, Shay picked on Elva to give up plumbing and go to work at Don's.

On Thursday, Shay opened a Styrofoam box of leftovers and started in. "Plumbing is insane. You should quit."

Elva leaned back on the couch and nibbled a hot wing. Her muscles throbbed. The sauce burned into a huge blister on her palm.

"Yuck. You need a hospital for that." Shay pointed at the gross-out blister. It hung like a baggy of water.

"It ain't so bad," Elva said.

"It looks awful." Shay gingerly pulled off her Keds and socks. Her big toe was cherry tomato red.

"At least my work boots protect my feet."

Their conversation died off. Elva went to bed early. The next day she received the miracle of her first wages.

"Don't spend it all in one damn place," Mr. Bob said, handing her a rubber-banded roll of cash— eight one-hundred dollar bills, a fifty, some ones. Papaw drove her to Prosperity Savings. She opened an account and got a temporary debit card.

"Too bad you won't be able to start spending," Papaw said when she climbed back into the truck.

"What you mean?" Elva asked.

"We work Saturday."

Tomorrow was the VFW Hall dance.

Elva dragged into work in the morning. She'd only have a little time to get ready for her date and thought about staying home.

"What do you need me to do first," Elva asked Yves when they reached the job site.

"Are you ready to try something new?"

Elva nodded and followed him to a worktable.

Yves held up a shiny U clamp.

"We have to fasten down the pipes," he said. "Every ten feet drill two holes, one inch to center on a girder, then fasten the clamps around the pipe with hex nuts."

"How about adding di-lithium crystals to those warp drives?" Elva murmured.

"Did you have a question, Hicks?"

"Could you demonstrate what you just said?" She stared at Yves boldly but could feel a muscle in her eyelid twitching.

"I'll do it one time." He marked a girder and drilled two holes. He inserted a clamp, and then tightened the hex nuts.

Elva nodded.

"You ready to quit?" Yves asked.

"Not hardly. Give me that drill." She put out a hand.

Yves barked out a high-pitched laugh. "You've got spark. I'll give you that. I'll check back later."

She squeezed the trigger on the drill and pointed at the girder. The motor revved and the drill bit flashed. She whipped out her tape measure and measured ten feet. She marked the girder and began to drill. The bit slid, making a scratch on the metal surface. She started again.

"More power to the engines, Scotty!" Elva shoved the bit against the girder. It slid off, again. Finally she created an indentation. She pushed harder. Almost. Almost.

The bit broke through. The drill ripped out of her hands! Shards of metal flew. The drill spun, hitting her fingers repeatedly. Elva yelped as the motor seized and stopped.

The knuckles on her right hand bled and a jagged scratch ran down her left forearm. She tried to yank the bit back through the hole she'd made, but it wouldn't budge.

Two arms encircled her. Wyatt.

She stiffened in shock as his heat poured though her clothes, and his rough calloused hands slid over her. He waited for her to catch her breath. She leaned into him. He smelled like—well, she didn't know it was possible to smell sexy.

"Flip the reverse arrow and pull the bit out," he said. His lips brushed her hair and his elbows brushed both her boobs as the bit easily backed out of the girder. He quickly punched a second hole.

"Keep at it." He inserted a clamp and walked away.

Elva fanned her burning face.

She wanted him, and she never wanted anything. Loser girls sat on the sidelines. But the plumbing was influencing her. Somehow, she'd stumbled out of the sidelines of life and into the game.

A surge of excess energy helped her drill the next two holes. The result was jagged and skewed, but she shoved in a clamp and tightened the hex nuts. Perfect.

One clamp down, a million to go.

When she got home, Elva was beyond dog-tired. Where would she find the strength for goat care and dancing? Nonny lounged in her chair in front of the TV. Elva pulled the milk jug out the fridge and took a huge swig.

"Did you take care of the goats?" Elva asked, wiping her face on her sleeve.

"No, but Shay's out there feeding them right now." Nonny smiled her gap-toothed grin.

Elva headed to the breezeway.

"I love babies," Shay crooned. Her hair was in

rollers and her nails had been manicured.

"You've saved me," Elva said.

"I know," Shay said. "I'll finish this, you get ready. Margarett and Chase will be here soon."

Full power to the warp engines. Elva took a quick bath in hotter-than-hell water. Her life was taking surprising turns toward freaking normal.

Elva's skin glowed lobster-red when Nonny tapped on the bathroom door and hollered, "Elva Presley, get your naked butt dressed. Margarett and her date are here."

Elva had long since resigned herself to a lifetime of embarrassment, but it still rankled.

"I'm coming." Elva changed into her spandex jeans, western shirt, and her Ropers. She'd bought the scuffed boots at a thrift shop in Houston. She brushed her hair and tapped on a straw cowboy hat with a glued-on tiara.

"Let's go dancing," she said, two-stepping into the living room. Nonny rested in her easy chair. Her giant pink muumuu billowed around her. Shay sat on the edge of the couch, wearing a t-shirt two sizes too small, Wranglers, and candy-red boots. A sparkly cowboy hat perched on her head.

Margarett stood by the door, grinning. Her bun was softer than usual and her purple jumper reached just below her knees instead of down to her ankles. Next to her, Chase Fleaso swung an arm around Margarett's bony shoulders. A week had passed since Chase had smacked Elva with that catfish kiss. God must be broadcasting a new message that centered on Margarett. Amen.

"Where's the concealer?" Elva asked.

"Here." Shay fumbled in her purse.

"Where are *our* dates?" Elva tried not to blink as Shay spread slick glop under her eye.

"The boys are meeting us at the Hall."

Elva checked out her eye in the mirror. The fading shiner was almost hidden.

"Let's go dancing." Elva leaned over the couch and pecked black velvet Elvis on the cheek.

Chase drove his dad's double cab truck. Margarett was glued to him like an appendage for the whole drive. The VFW Hall parking lot was packed with pickups, and Chase parked in two spaces so no one would dent the doors.

"There're the boys." Shay pointed at two men standing in the doorway of the Hall. One was the guy Shay worked with at the truck stop.

"Those guys are a million years old." Elva coughed. "We can't date them. It's got to be illegal."

"We're just here to dance." Shay hopped out of the truck and waved. "Howdy, boys."

Elva turned to ask Chase to drive her home, but, lo' and behold, Margarett was sucking catfish breath out of Chase. They wouldn't be driving home anytime soon.

"The boys are waiting," Shay said.

Nothing to do but go all in, Elva thought. She followed Shay to the door.

"Nice to meet you," Elva said, putting out a hand to the guy who worked at Don's.

He tapped his straw hat. "Bobby Ray."

She put her hand out to the other man. He had black hair, a sloppy mustache, and was ancient, maybe even thirty.

"I'm David Esparza." His silver tipped boot thumped into the pavement, and he grinned—a smarmy, brown recluse spider crawling-all-over-you smile.

Elva took a cleansing breath and centered herself.

She could do this. She'd watched enough *Star Trek* to know how to face unusual life forms and first contact situations.

Elva took another look and wished she were of age to drink.

"Let's dance," she said, and hooked an arm around Mr. Esparza's, pulling him into the Hall.

An hour later they were circling the dance floor with disappointing results. Elva tried not to yelp every time his silver-tipped boots stamped down on her toes. They polkaed, two-stepped, and joined in a couple of line dances. She kept wondering if her big toenail would slough off. Mr. Esparza had stomped on it an unlucky thirteen times.

During the band's second set, Mr. Esparza decided to make his move. He waltzed Elva into a dark hallway off the dance floor.

"I'm not ready to stop dancing," Elva said, though beading sweat had formed on her forehead.

"You've got curves in all the right places." Mr. Esparza placed a strategic hand over her backside, and the other groped her boob.

Mr. Esparza apparently didn't listen.

"Let's go out to my truck and get it on." His hot breath curled inside her ear.

"I'm sixteen-years-old," Elva said, her voice flat and emotionless. She was really seventeen, but she was no fool.

"What the hell?" Mr. Esparza's hands slid off her boob and butt like they'd been stuck in battery acid. "I can't risk my parole."

"Right. I'm going to find my friends and go home now." Elva backed out of the hallway. She scanned the dance floor until she spied Shay and Bobby Ray locked in a slow dance and walked across the smooth plank floor to tap Shay's shoulder.

"I want to go home," Elva said. "Now."

"I'm not ready to leave," Shay said. "Dancing doesn't end for another hour."

Elva tried a different tactic.

"Do you know how old she is?" Elva asked Bobby Ray.

"Old enough to know what she wants," Bobby Ray answered. His smile was worse than scummy—scuzzy.

"Sixteen for another twelve weeks," Elva said.

The absolute truth. Bobby Ray paled under the string lights of the Hall.

"She's so funny." Shay took Bobby Ray's arm and gave him a dazzling smile. Bobby Ray looked visibly relieved.

Idiot.

"I'm finding Chase and Margarett and heading home," Elva said. "You ought to come with us." She saw Margarett and Chase at a table over by the bar. "I'll see you later."

Elva left Shay hanging on Bobby Ray's arm, passing a Cerveza sign and a row of kegs beside the bar. Chase and Margarett held hands over a small table. She had to admit they were sweet, like a whole tub of Betty Crocker cream cheese frosting spread on saltines.

"I need to go," Elva said. "I've got work tomorrow."

"I guess we can drive you," Chase said.

"I don't want to go yet," Margarett protested.

This was probably the first taste of sinful freedom Margarett had ever had.

"Do your parents know that you're out with a boy?" Elva ignored the twinge of guilt from spoiling Margarett's pleasure.

"You're not going to tell?" Margarett asked.

"Not ever," Elva said. "But I need to get home, and you don't need to get caught."

Margarett nodded, standing. "Mama won't suspect anything if I come home early."

"Elva, you're all right." Chase stood up and gave Margarett a squeeze and a kiss.

Elva didn't answer. What was she supposed to say? Of course she was all right. She was fabulous, awesome, wonderful, and too good for him.

She followed Chase and Margarett outside. She checked out Chase's round butt on the way. Chase had his good points. His butt wasn't one of them.

In the truck, she popped a breath mint and stared out the window. Stars stretched from horizon to horizon in the inky night sky. Margarett giggled and scooted closer to Chase.

"I'm posting our fanfic as soon as I get a laptop," Elva said.

"Elva, Chase doesn't want to hear about our stories. It's kid's stuff."

"What's she talking about?" Chase squeezed Margarett's shoulders.

"Fanfic," Elva said. "We've been writing *Trek* stories since the seventh grade.

"I like *Star Trek* too," Chase said. "The *Enterprise* series is my favorite. I really love that song at the beginning." To Elva's horror Chase began to sing.

"There's deep faith in my heart …"

"Is that Christian?" Margarett asked. "Elva, why didn't you tell me there was a Christian *Star Trek*?"

Elva choked on her breath mint. Those weren't even the words.

"Can we write an *Enterprise* story?" Margarett asked.

"I'd like to try that," Chase said.

Was he trying to take over their fanfic group?

"We only write classic Trek." Elva said in a no-nonsense monotone.

"Couldn't we just try—" Margarett said.

Elva cut in. "No, we can't. So how is slicing hunks of ham and chopping up chickens?"

A change of subject was absolutely necessary.

"It's going really good," Margarett said. "I'm learning how to use fillet knives."

"We can talk about *Trek* later," Chase said.

Chase *was* trying to take over the fanfic group!

Elva almost growled. Classic *Star Trek* had kept the Loser Girls afloat since the seventh grade. The seventh grade! The abomination *Enterprise* series would corrupt the flow, the meaning, the adventure of all their fanfic. Margarett dating a pig farmer was ruining everything. Everything!

"Illogical." Spock would say. "Illogical, Jim."

11 HEAT STROKE

Rap. Rap. Rap.

Elva sat up with a start. Bleary eyed, she looked at the clock, four in the morning. Someone knocked on her window again. Hadn't Shay heard of a door?

"Shay, come on in." Elva yawned and stretched.

The window popped opened. "It ain't Shay. It's Margarett." Margarett shoved a laundry basket of clothes through the window and then grabbed at the headboard. She pulled herself inside.

Elva swung her feet off the bed. "What are you doing here?"

"Daddy threw me out."

"What?" Elva shook her head in an attempt to clear the cobwebs.

"He caught me necking with Chase in the pickup. He didn't say anything until Chase had driven away." Margarett's voice cracked. "Daddy called me a loose woman and told me I didn't have a home anymore. He shoved all my stuff in this basket and set it out on the porch. I walked here." Margarett eased off her flip-flops. Huge red blisters had formed between her toes. Elva shook her head. Margarett's daddy wasn't worth two cents.

"Why didn't you call Chase?"

"Chase keeps my cell phone. Daddy thinks a cell phone is the work of the devil. I came here because your house is closest."

"I got Band-aids for your feet," Elva said as soothing as possible. "Do you want me to call Chase now?"

"I can't sleep over at Chase's. That would be a sin."

Elva raised an eyebrow. If anyone needed some sin in her life it was Margarett, but her friend wasn't ready for that much truth.

"I don't think Shay is coming home tonight," Elva said. "You can take the couch."

"Where's Shay?" Margarett asked.

"Oh, I expect she went home." Elva answered with a bald lie, but Margarett wouldn't understand that Shay was off with Bobby Ray. Thankfully, Margarett accepted Elva's explanation and headed into the living room. Elva pulled her pillow over her head and rolled over.

The next day, Margarett went to church with Chase, and Elva lazed around. Shay called to say she'd be gone another day.

On Monday, the alarm clock buzzed at an ungodly hour. Elva groaned and swung out of bed. She passed Margarett snoring on the couch and headed out to feed the goats. A humid blast hit her face. A scorching heat wave had begun over the weekend. The high in Houston would break records.

The heat at the valve plant slowed her down and set her on edge as she endlessly drilled and clamped.

"You haven't done much this morning, Elva." Wyatt's breath was against her neck. "It's lunchtime already. We're not leaving until we've finished this section."

Elva jerked. Damn. The drill bit snapped off.

"Be careful," Wyatt said. "You could hurt someone."

"I'm working like hell." Elva's words growled out of her.

"Calm down, wildcat." Wyatt leaned on the girder and took the drill out of her hands. His face dripped with sweat and his shirt was stuck to his stomach.

Elva swiped her forehead. Her hair was sopping wet from sweat. The oppressive heat made it difficult to breathe. Clamminess and lightheadedness hit her at the same time. Wyatt half-smiled at her, and she answered by vomiting on their boots. He stepped back, and she continued to heave. Finally the heaves slowed to a few dry coughs.

"Drink this." Wyatt held up a water bottle.

Elva took it gratefully. "Thanks."

"You need to stay hydrated in this heat. Let's get you out of here and into the shade outside." He gently took her elbow and guided her through the big hanger doors.

A welcome breeze brushed her face. Wyatt led her around the building, and she collapsed under a scrubby tree.

"Wait here." Wyatt disappeared back around the building.

She snapped off her hard hat and put her face on her knees, wobbling like a plate of cherry Jell-O. Wyatt came back with an entire water cooler and a brown paper sack. He stopped next to her and popped the top off the cooler. He poured out some water, splashing the vomit off her shoes. How did he keep so clean? He still smelled fresh, like sun-dried sheets.

Elva coughed when he dumped water on her head. He scooped one more cup over his own head. Cool water dripped across her lips, salty, refreshing. He spilled another cup on her back. The water trickled down her spine in the most delicious way. Nothing had ever felt as good.

"Do you want a sandwich?" He squatted down and opened the paper sack again. "Turkey on rye or roast beef on wheat?"

"I'll take the turkey," Elva said.

He handed her the sandwich and a bag of

Doritos.

She held out the five dollar bill that she kept tucked in her sock.

"Keep your lunch money," he said.

Elva took the sandwich and chips gratefully. Hunger gnawed inside her even though she'd just spewed her stomach contents out. She unwrapped the brown squashed square and tore out a huge bite, not bothering to chew. Her taste buds were still shocked from leftover traces of vomit. Still, Wyatt had paid for her lunch and somehow that made this the best sandwich ever. She tore open the bag of Doritos and munched the salty heavenly pieces.

"Whoa," Wyatt said. "Take it easy there, gal. You need to eat slower, or you're going to toss your whole lunch back on my shoes again."

"OK." Elva's next bite was almost dainty, slowly chewed. "Why are you being so nice to me?" She squinted.

Wyatt ignored her. "You need to drink a cup of water every hour. If you don't stay hydrated, you might end up in the hospital, and our insurance is crap. You'd have to pay the whole thing out of pocket."

"OK, I'll remember," Elva said.

Wyatt stuffed his sandwich in his mouth. "Yves wants you back, installing clamps in ten minutes. Don't give him a reason to lose his temper because then he's not fit to live with today. Damn heat." Wyatt put his hands on his thighs and stood up.

"Wyatt?"

"Yes?" He gazed down his nose at her.

"You got a phone?" Elva asked. Somewhere inside her a surge of boldness erupted.

"I do."

"Can I borrow it?" she asked. "I've got to call Nonny and my friend Shay."

Wyatt reached into his pocket, pulling his jeans even tighter around his hips. He tossed it to her.

"Keep it 'til quitting time," he said.

"What happens if somebody calls?" Elva asked.

"Let 'em leave a message," he said and sauntered away. She took a last sideways glance at him as he rounded the warehouse. He had such a fine, awesome butt. She slid the phone in her pocket, crunched another Dorito, and dripped some more water on her face.

12 THE WYATT INCIDENT

Elva had never used a phone with a touch screen before. She resisted every urge to read Wyatt's text messages. She opened his *Angry Birds* app by accident and then finally figured everything out and called Nonny, but her grandmother didn't pick up. Next she tried Margarett.

She left a voice message. "You remember the cute guy at work? We had a moment. He bought me lunch. This is his phone."

Then she tried Shay. Elva was leaving a voice message when the phone beeped.

Can't ansr my phone. @ wrk. Shay texted. *Is this your phone?*

Elva hunted and pecked out her answer.

Hot guy's phone. He bought me lunch.

Whoa, talk later. Details. Got2go.

Elva stared at the messages in horror. Lord, Wyatt would see them when she gave the phone back. She had to delete them now! She tapped desperately for a while and breathed a sigh of relief when she swiped the text and a delete button popped up.

"Hicks, what in the hell are you doing?" Yves asked.

Elva twitched. "Making some calls."

"Damn it! I expected you on the job ten minutes ago." Yves' pitchy whine made her skin crawl. He'd pulled off his t-shirt exposing a huge dragon tattoo emblazoned on his protruding potbelly. His arms bulged and his eyes were bloodshot.

"I'm coming." Elva stood and stretched. "It won't happen again."

"Damn straight," Yves said. "You're Old Man Hicks's granddaughter and all, but I'll fire your sorry ass if I ever catch you wasting time again." He kicked the dirt away.

Elva nodded. The dang hypocrite was strung out on weed.

She returned to the roasting building. Her arms ached as she drilled. The buzz dug into her head. Her back was stiff. Several new bruises formed around the many older ones on her arms. The cups of water she'd drunk sloshed around in her stomach. Later, the building started to thin out, and her drilling grew slower and slower. The welders left, and so did the electricians. Only a few scattered workers remained in the cavernous space.

Cece Barlow

The lowering sun stretched a long swath of orange light into the plant. The emptiness made the sound of her drill echo loudly. Her eyes kept drifting downward. Who knew you could fall asleep drilling?

"Elva?" It was Wyatt. "It's time to close up shop."

Elva let go of the drill's trigger. Her arms were weighted like heavy logs. She leaned against one of the plant's vertical girders. Wyatt had to pry the drill out of her rigid fingers.

"You know about plumbing, don't you?" he asked as he rolled up the electrical cord.

"Know what?" She stretched her shaking fingers. The girder was the only thing holding up her jelly legs.

"The first weeks are hell." He unclipped the plastic strap of her hard hat. "It's downhill from there."

Elva met his smiling eyes, crinkling at the corners.

"That's the first good news I've heard all day," she said.

Wyatt laughed. "I like you, Elva Presley." His hand slid up one of her hips and pinched her waist. A *GQ* Hottie liked her, and he had a good butt. He wasn't a scary guy who weighed a million pounds and raised pigs. He was hot and steamy and everything. This felt better than when Papaw gave her a Lotto scratch card, and she'd won $100.

"Are you coming, Elva?" Wyatt had moved toward the wide double doors.

"Yeah." Elva reached for her coffee can of drill bits and clamps on the floor. Her back creaked as she bent over.

"You can leave that stuff," Wyatt said. "I already put the coolers away for you."

"Thanks." Elva yawned. She'd never been so tired. She was about to sink down on the floor when Wyatt's arm came around her again.

"Keep moving, honey." He guided her out of the building. The sky had turned Louisiana Iris purple. Yves joined them.

"Hicks looks half-dead," Yves said. "I'll lock up the other trailer."

Yves never offered to help her. Elva looked at him in bleary-eyed surprise. He tossed the truck keys to Wyatt. "You're driving."

In the truck, Elva slumped in the middle of the bench seat. Wyatt shifted his arm to rest against her shoulders. She was too tired to fully appreciate the contact.

On the trip back to the plumbing shop, she was mesmerized by miles of tan-colored of freeway lit by freeway lights. Her eyelids kept sliding downward. When they came to stop at the plumbing shop, Elva's head rested on Wyatt's shoulder and drool had slopped on his shirt.

He didn't say anything but wiped the corner of her lips with his thumb.

A chill of excitement mixed in with her sleepiness.

"Wyatt, stay with Hicks until her old man shows

up." Yves was filling out the daily timesheet on his small industrial touchpad. "Damn, we've put in fifteen hours today."

Yves stuffed the pad in the glove compartment and stumbled out of the work truck to his beat-up Ford. It squealed out of the parking lot.

Elva kept her eyes closed. She listened to Wyatt's slow breaths and became aware of the beats of her heart. Whoosh. Bump. Whoosh.

"You're a real restful gal," Wyatt said.

Her brain addled from weariness, Elva didn't twitch when Wyatt laced his fingers with hers. He slowly reeled her around so she was facing him. He slid an arm behind her back and splayed his fingers across her thigh. Finally, she was going to have a proper first kiss.

He lifted her chin. His lips touched hers. He tasted of onion and bologna, and his lips were thinner and smaller than she'd imagined. The stick shift dug into her back and the steering wheel cut into her side with stabbing pain. She would have moved away, but his hand slid under her shirt. His mouth smashed her lips open, and he began licking around inside her mouth. He really, really needed a breath mint, but she was curious. He unhooked her bra and squeezed her breast in a more awkward way than sexy. Was this supposed to be hot? Or did she just not know how to react? He grabbed her hand, resting on his waist, and pushed it downward. She touched an alarming bulge.

"Undo my pants, honey," Wyatt said.

Elva froze. She sucked in a breath at this full-speed-to-the-warp-engines move.

She shoved against his chest. "Hey, Wyatt, stop."

"What the hell?" He pinched her breast. "Come, on. It'll just take a second."

"I'm just not ready." Elva pushed away his hand. This was certainly not the bliss that Nonny had told her about. Wasn't pinching her breast supposed to feel special? Instead it hurt like heck. He'd moved too far, too fast.

"Stop!" Elva's voice was frantic.

Wyatt spat a vile curse and hit the dash. Elva scrambled to the far side of the cab. She reached back to rehook her bra. This first-contact situation had gone wrong, very wrong.

"It's your loss." He ran his fingers through his hair and hit the steering wheel again, spewing even more disgusting words.

"I'm sorry," Elva whispered. "Papaw's coming. You should probably just go."

"You don't know what you'll be missing," Wyatt said. He reached for her. Elva stiffened as his fingers slipped down her side to her hip into her pocket. He pulled out his cell phone. She breathed a sigh of relief.

"If you ever change your mind, let me know," he said, reaching behind the seat for his helmet. "I'm outta here."

"OK, bye," Elva said.

She watched as he gunned away on his motorcycle, then she stumbled out of the truck and sank down cross-legged on the warm curb. A wave of adrenaline kept her heart pounding. What had just happened? They'd rounded first base to second, and headed out to third in less than five minutes.

She hardly knew Wyatt.

They'd had a spark, but this was totally unexpected, exciting, and yet kind of awful. She wanted to explore the pleasures, that's what Nonny called them, but this wasn't what she had thought would happen. It was supposed to be magic and heaven. This had been beyond stupid.

Elva crossed her arms over her breasts. Had she really touched him? She didn't know whether to laugh or cry. Did the painful squeeze in her heart and the roaring in her ears mean she was in love? Lust? Was she madder than hell? Flattered? She didn't know.

She pressed her hands to her hot cheeks.

In *Star Trek*, making out was always effortless— the kisses, the touches, it was all perfect. Real life was way more complicated. This first experiment, testing of the waters, hadn't been what she had hoped, but she wanted to try again.

One sure thing, the Wyatt incident had allowed embers of hope for a normal life to spring up in her soul like wild grass after a soaking rain.

13 DEBRIEF

She powered up her computer when she got home. The Wyatt incident had scraped her emotions raw. Elva had to work them out.

Her crunching computer finally opened up her fanfic file, and she considered the next scene. It begged for more reality. T'Pak was involved with an alien life form and wondering whether to step things up a notch. The Gorn Prince would move first, overwhelming T'Pak with a startling ritual sex move. Elva typed furiously.

His forked lizard tongue swathed T'Pak's face.

"Stop, Prince Vol." T'Pak protested strongly. She coughed and swiped at the sticky goo dripping off her cheek.

Prince Vol flipped his tail suggestively and

powerfully, roughing up the tender skin on T'Pak's stomach.

Elva leaned back her head. This section burst with lifelike energy, sending shivers down her back. T'Pak revealed displeasure, and the Prince responded with the right amount of anger. But were the motivations of her characters balanced? T'Pak wasn't in ponfarr, the mating season for Vulcans, so she couldn't properly respond to the advances of the handsome lizard. Gorns also emitted odd smells for sensitive Vulcan senses, and Elva had yet to address that.

She knew how to close the scene. The Prince would apologize, admitting T'Pak's beauty had overwhelmed him. Elva tapped her cheek. Would T'Pak she give him another chance?

Of course.

Her best story to date.

Elva rubbed her hands together. She glanced at her clock. When would Shay be home from work? Hopefully before Margarett. She wanted to discuss the Wyatt incident, but not with Margarett.

Lord, the house seemed like a sauna. She dropped an ice cube down her shirt.

"Hey, Elva." Shay lifted the window and climbed through onto the bed. She swung off her backpack.

"I've been waiting and waiting," Elva said. "I've got way more Wyatt news."

"I'd love to talk, but I don't have much time."

Shay pulled out a couple of plastic garbage bags from her backpack and began to shove her pile of clothes into one.

"Where are you going?"

"Bobby Ray and I have decided to take our relationship to the next level."

"What level is that?" Elva asked.

"We're moving into his travel trailer together."

"Are you sure you're ready for that?" Elva asked.

"A woman knows." Shay patted Elva's hand like she was a child.

Right then Nonny waddled up to the door. "That boy is too old for you, Missy. Does your mama know what you're doing?"

Elva chewed on the inside of her cheek. Part of her wished Nonny would hush and let Shay get into whatever trouble she pleased, but another part of her agreed with Nonny. Moving in with Bobby Ray seemed like buying a used car sight unseen. What did Shay know about Bobby Ray anyway?

"Nonny, everybody lives together these days," Shay said.

"That boy's brainwashing you, telling you what you want to hear." Nonny took a bite of a moonpie. "You need to find a boy nearer your age."

"Nonny, your muumuu is sure pretty," Elva said. "Why are you so dressed up?" She put full power to changing the subject. This conversation had to be stopped.

Nonny smoothed down her patterned tent dress. "My friend, Myra, is driving me into town to play midnight bingo up at the Hall. We're dropping by the Wal-Mart. Do you need anything, Elva?"

"No, I'm good." Elva saved her file and powered down her computer. *Star Trek* would wait. Shay dove under the bed for her flip-flops.

A horn honked outside.

"There's Myra," Nonny said. "I'll be back in later." She turned to Elva. "I left more moonpies on the table." Nonny planted a kiss on Elva's cheek and then left.

"I can't wait for Bobby Ray to get here," Shay said. "He loves me."

"Did he say that?" Elva asked.

Shay tossed the rest of her stuff into the second bag: underwear, a tattered robe, small bags of toiletries and make-up went into the garbage bag. She dragged both into the living room. "Not in so many words, but we don't need words."

Elva followed her, hauling Shay's backpack. She didn't know what to say. How could you love somebody and not tell them?

"Are you sure you want this?" Elva asked.

"Of course, this is what I want," Shay said, sitting on the couch. "Why ask a thing like that?"

"Because I'm your friend. I watch out for the Loser Girls." Elva joined her.

"That's a stupid name," Shay said.

"Maybe. But it's always us against the Universe, and I bet on us. I'm not sure Bobby Ray is what you want."

"Why would you say that, Elva?"

"I want you to find good things." Elva hugged a throw pillow.

"Then be happy for me," Shay said.

Elva sighed and then said, "All right." But in truth, a wave of unhappiness crashed over her. Shay was messing up. They sat on the couch side by side. The Elvis clock in the kitchen filled in the silence with the even-paced tick-tick-tick of its swinging legs.

"I guess Bobby Ray is taking longer than he said," Shay said. "Tell me what happened with Wyatt."

Elva let off a deep breath. Finally, a chance to talk about the Wyatt incident. She launched right in.

"We kinda made out in his truck."

"Did anything really happen?" Shay opened her make-up bag and began organizing her lipsticks and shadows.

"He kissed me ... a lot." Elva started to break down the details, but Shay jumped in with a question.

"When did he kiss you?"

"After work," Elva said.

"So you work together all the time?" Shay shoveled her lipsticks into a Ziploc bag.

Elva nodded.

"Were you alone for a while? "

"Yeah," Elva said.

"Then it probably isn't anything. Stuff happens."

Shay shoved the shadows back in her makeup bag. "Don't read too much into this guy. You haven't even been on a date with him, have you?"

"But—" Elva protested.

Shay put up her palm. "I have WAY more experience than you."

"Yes, but—"

"No buts. He's just flirting."

"It was more than flirting," Elva said, though a voice inside her whispered Shay was right.

A shrill horn sounded outside.

"Maybe," Shay said. "I'd love to hear everything, but Bobby Ray is waiting."

"Let me tell you a bit more." Elva said.

Shay waved her off. "I don't have time to pick this apart. Call me later." Shay headed out to Bobby Ray.

Elva marched into her bedroom and flung herself down on the bed with a thump. Shay had acted like Wyatt's kisses were nothing. Those kisses were something, they were! Shay's attitude sliced her and opened a wound. Did Wyatt even like her? Was Shay right? Elva desperately needed to talk some more. She jumped up and grabbed the phone in the kitchen, and punched in Shay's number.

Leave a message after the tone.

Beep.

"Shay, pick up. I still need to talk." But Shay didn't pick up, even after Elva left a half-dozen voice messages. There was no answer and there wouldn't be. Shay was headed out on an out-of-control freight train called Bobby Ray.

Finally, Elva grudgingly called Margarett, but there was no answer there either. She left a message. Talking to Margarett was a stupid idea anyway. Shay had serious experience. Margarett only had Chase and God. Elva didn't need the Wyatt incident poured through that filter.

Later, there was a tap on the window.

"You really need a cell phone." Margarett climbed through and tossed her backpack on the bed. "I've got a ton of text messages for you from Shay."

"I left voicemail," Elva said. "She should call."

Margarett sat on the bed and began to extract her hair from her hair net. "Nobody calls, Elva. People text."

Margarett handed Elva her phone. Elva read the string of texts. They repeated in the following order:

Bobby Ray's hotness is supernova!

I don't have a free second to talk.

ELVA HAD BETTER GET HER OWN CELL PHONE ASAP.

Elva swallowed hard. Her Mac dream had to go on pause until she had her own cell phone tucked into the back pocket of her jeans.

The whole Wyatt incident proved her desperate need.

"I'll get the goat bottles ready." Margarett untied her Dr. Scholl's shoes and rubbed her feet on the wood floor. "So tell me about this boy, Wyatt."

"The goats! Oh no, I about forgot them. My karma can't take a black mark from goat neglect." Why, oh why, had she told Margarett about Wyatt?

"Karma's of the devil," Margarett said, following Elva into the kitchen. "It sounds like you and Wyatt have a thing going. What exactly happened?"

"Not much," Elva said, carrying one bottle. Margarett carried the others.

"Do you think Wyatt is in love with you? Is he a Christian?" Margarett fired questions, lifting a goat onto her lap. "Do you want to marry him and have his babies?"

What the heck? Elva bit her tongue to keep from snapping at clueless Margarett. She did the only thing she could think of to move Margarett away from the Wyatt incident.

"How's Chase?" she asked.

And Margarett launched into the praises of her pig farmer.

"Chase is fantastic. He took me to a hog auction. That's why I was so late. He's taking me to a movie tomorrow. He's going to buy me buttered popcorn, Coke, and Red Vines. I've never been to a movie before.

Elva patted Nurse Chapel's belly, and the baby burped.

"Wow, Margarett, aren't movies of the devil." Elva let the flaming arrow fly. Margarett was so dang happy.

"Chase set me straight." Margarett fed Bones, totally missing the snarkiness. "Only the Rs are from the devil, PGs are fine in moderation."

"Good to know," Elva replied and picked up M'Benga.

"But enough about me," Margarett said. "Tell me more about your Wyatt."

"He bought me lunch," Elva said. "And kissed me after work." She didn't mention which bases they'd covered. Margarett would take those details as an opportunity to launch into a purity pledge pitch.

"He sounds nice," Margarett said. "But I've something important to talk about—the Lifeway Food Bank Annual Pancake Supper is coming up, our annual tradition. Chase plans to pick me up at work on Saturday around five. We can pick you up here after that."

What? Margarett was glossing over the Wyatt incident like it was nothing! What?

What!

"I might not need a ride," Elva said in a calculated off-hand way. She didn't need charity. Wyatt kind of liked her; she was sure. "Wyatt might bring me. I'm planning to ask him to go with me."

Elva crossed her fingers behind her back. He'd go. Probably.

"If it don't work out, Chase and I will still take you," Margarett said. "You can let me know if anything changes."

"I'm pretty sure he'll say yes," Elva said.

Buzzz. Margarett's phone vibrated.

"I've got to take this." Margarett said "We can talk about Wyatt later." Margarett went back in the house to chat privately. Elva picked up Bones, hugging the small goat. He smelled of hay and stale formula.

"At least you'll listen to me," Elva whispered in his satiny pink ear.

14 THE RED SHIRT

"Elva, get out of that danged bed." Papaw's voice boomed on Friday morning. "I won't be late."

The week had passed quickly and everyday Elva tried to get up her nerve to ask Wyatt to the pancake supper, but she'd failed. She hobbled across the hardwood floor, like an old woman. Her shoulders ached already. Elva reached for a bottle of ibuprofen and swallowed two pills without a sip of water.

The purple-black sky glowed warm red on the eastern horizon when they left. Papaw turned on the highway. The air was already disturbingly hot and humid, and bugs swarmed in the headlights, thumping against the windshield. Elva slid back into the oblivion of sleep.

"Wake up, gal." Papaw shook her shoulder.

They were pulling into the shop, and her face was mashed up against the window.

"OK." She blinked, trying to come awake. The truck stopped, and she almost fell when the door swung open. Her face peeled off the window with a painful pricking of her skin.

"Morning, Elva." She caught a flash of Wyatt's white teeth and his tan Stetson.

Elva swung her feet to the ground. Wyatt reached out to steady her. Both of his hands rested on her shoulders. She closed her eyes, luxuriating in the moment. Really, all she and Wyatt needed was time to get know each other, and then she'd be ready to explore more. Should she ask him to the supper now?

Wyatt gave her a hard shake. "C'mon, wake up, Hicks."

The moment was gone.

"Let's go," Yves said. "We're late."

He said that every day. Plumbing created a kind of temporal loop. Each day merged into the next with only the slightest of variations.

She set-up the water jugs and installed clamps. Through the day, Elva tried to muse about the next twist in her fanfic. Occasionally, a promising thought turned over, but these moments were few. Mostly her thoughts streamed out like white noise.

It was still early when Wyatt told her to close up shop.

"Is it really quitting time?" Elva asked.

"Naw," Wyatt said. "But Yves has a concert

tonight, and we've got to pick up our paychecks."

Elva cleaned up her area and headed out to the truck. She still hadn't asked Wyatt to the supper. She leaned against the hood but yelped. The metal burned hot enough to fry an egg.

Wyatt walked up. "Too hot for you to handle?" And then he winked at her.

This was it. The moment.

"Wyatt, I was wondering if you'd like to go with me—"

Yves interrupted. "Time to pick up the paychecks."

Dang, she couldn't ask Wyatt with Yves right there.

A half-hour later, a wintry blast of AC hit them when they opened the door to the Carus office. Master Plumber Mr. Bob jerked awake in the easy chair.

"Shut the damn door," Mr. Bob said, growling and sputtering. He instantly calmed when it closed, and he became a wise Buddha, imparting sage advice. "Payday's on Friday. Damn most important thing to know." He flipped through a stack of envelopes and handed one to Yves and another to Wyatt.

"How do you like plumbing?" Mr. Bob asked Elva, handing her a rubber-banded wad of cash that Uncle Sam wouldn't be able to track.

"Fine." Elva flushed with pride. How many went to plumbing Hell and survived?

"Has she done her work?" Mr. Bob asked Yves.

"She's slow," Yves said.

"She tries hard." Wyatt put in.

"She does do that," Yves said.

Elva thumbed through the thick stack of bills. It smelled like a pinch of ink, a bite of cigar smoke, and a gallon of the clean, heavenly smell of financial freedom.

Papaw ducked his head in the door.

"Dammit, you're letting out the damn air conditioning," Mr. Bob growled.

Papaw ignored Mr. Bob. "Elva, do you want to put your money in the bank?"

"I do," Elva said. "And I need to stop by Wal-Mart to fill Nonny's Zoloft prescription."

"I'll see you tomorrow morning," Yves said. "We're working the whole weekend."

"We work the whole weekend." Elva parroted.

There was no possibility of a date with Wyatt. None! She rushed out of the office and around the shop, to a toolbox on the backside of the building. She collapsed on it and took gulping breaths. She hadn't realized until this moment how much she had been counting on the supper.

Dang tears. She swiped at them. She sure wasn't going to let anyone see her crying.

The loss cut deep. She wanted to go, more than she'd realized. She never got what she wanted.

She started in surprise when Wyatt joined her on the box. He leaned in close. His garlicky breath tickled her shoulder. He smelled of sweat and salt. She rubbed her nose.

"Hon, we're working without breaks right now." Wyatt swung an arm around her. "Didn't anyone tell you?"

"Not a word. I was going out with my friends this weekend." Elva sniffed.

"Pretty gal like you should be going out." Wyatt kissed her temple. "I'm sorry." He placed a hand on her thigh. "Maybe we can work something out. We'll get you home early."

"You will?" Elva asked.

"If I have to." He smiled. "I'll take you home on my bike."

If he drove her home, why couldn't he come to the supper with her? This was it—her chance. "Wyatt, I want to ask you something."

"Ain't she young for you?" Yves stepped around the corner, laughing. Wyatt's hands jumped off her thigh like he was touching a piece of sheet metal in the hot Texas sun.

Behind Yves was Papaw, frowning. His face had turned bright red.

Wyatt stood without a word and hurried to his bike. Papaw glared at him. Wyatt fumbled for his helmet and then kick-started the engine. He didn't glance at Elva as he rolled past. At the corner, he stopped and yelled back something at the crew, gesturing at her. She was too far away to hear his words but could hear the laughter, Mr. Bob, and the whole crew joining in. Papaw shook his head and gave her a fierce stare, like this was her fault.

"Elva, get in the dang truck!" Papaw's voice

cracked with emotion.

Elva stared down at the blacktop parking lot. Papaw was trying to protect her in his old Texas way. She also understood the crew's laughter. Wyatt had yelled something crass about her, his purpose crystal clear. She didn't mean a thing to him.

She glanced down at her t-shirt, a red one. In *Star Trek* the guy in a red shirt was sprayed by killer flowers or incinerated with death rays from an alien probe. Nothing good came his way. She was the expendable *Star Trek* ensign

.

15 HARLEY RIDE

The shock of Wyatt's cruelty reverberated in her molecules. Elva climbed in Papaw's truck, aching for a premature cancellation to her plumbing days, but the money, she couldn't lose a whole mountain of money. She thumped the dash with her fist.

"Don't hit my dang truck," Papaw said. That's the only thing he said on the whole drive home and in a way Elva was grateful. She tore into the house the second they stopped, and she grabbed for her fanfic. She copied the whole file to a memory stick and then went to Nonny. Papaw was holed up in his bedroom. He didn't want to talk.

"Nonny, will you go with me to the library?" Elva begged. "There's enough time before they close. I'll drive." She had to counteract the Wyatt humiliation by doing something positive. Who did he think he was anyway? She could do better. She could do way better. He didn't know what he was missing.

"Elva, I'm feeling too puny for town." Nonny tucked her Elvis throw under her arms.

"Aren't we out of Doritos and Mountain Dew?" Nonny couldn't survive without her Habanero-hot Doritos and Dew. "I'll buy some."

Nonny paused and then nodded. "I guess we can go for a while."

"Good." Elva offered Nonny her house shoes. "You can visit your friends while I'm at the library, and then we can go to Wal-Mart. I'll buy you a Big Mac Meal at the McDonalds, too." Nonny had a particular fondness for Big Macs.

"I'll get dressed," Nonny said.

Score. Elva pumped her arm. She'd print out the entire manuscript with the library's printer. And for more therapy, she'd buy a cell phone at Wally World.

In town, she dropped off Nonny at a friend's house and headed to the library. Mrs. Cook looked the other way when Elva went ten pages over the library's free print limit. Power coursed through her veins. She tapped the stack against the table, loving the feel of actual pages against her fingers. She rubber-banded the stack and zipped back for Nonny.

"Are you ready for Wal-Mart?" Elva asked as her grandmother got in the truck.

"Sounds good," Nonny said.

Elva turned the air conditioning vents on her face, letting the blast of cold hit her as she drove to Wal-Mart. A cell phone, oh, so tangible, oh, so life affirming—it was about to be hers.

She settled Nonny with her Big Mac Meal in the McDonald's at the front of the store and headed to the electronics section in the back. She passed the laptops but wasn't tempted one bit. A no-name laptop wasn't good enough. Her laptop would be a Mac from an Apple Store and that would cost major $$$$.

It took Elva only a few minutes to pick out a shiny new phone with a pay-as-you-go plan. Shay would be the inaugural call. Margarett was working behind the butcher's counter and after work was heading to Friday night church; she wouldn't pick up. Yes, Margarett was still attending Holiness, totally bananas.

Elva texted Shay.

Amazingly, Shay called her right back. "Hey, Elva I'm on break." Excessive static crackled on the line; people shouted in the background.

"I bought my new cell phone." Elva's words shot out like hornets. "I can't wait for the pancake supper."

"Is Wyatt coming?" Shay's voice notched up, rising over the din.

"That's still up in the air." Elva couldn't admit there was no way he was coming.

"I hope it works out," Shay said. More noise followed. "Dang, it's busy. I have to go, I'll see you tomorrow." Her words were muffled by the twang of Western music. A sure click followed her quick, "Bye."

"See you," Elva said into the cold silence. The screen on her new cell phone was smudged, and she rubbed the surface with the corner of her shirt. She took a deep cleansing breath, paddling back into the safe waters of thankfulness. Regardless of the widening gulf between her and her friends, one good thing continued flooding her life, plumbing cash.

She had buying power.

They headed home and after dinner, she fed the sleepy kids while Nonny watched a mystery show. Papaw snored like a buzz saw in the bedroom. Once the kids were taken care of, Elva applied a new rhinestone bling kit to her phone. The stones winked in the light from the lamp by her bed. She wished someone would call. Elva sighed and opened her phone to Margarett.

Margo, wrking 2morrow, but pick me up for the supper @ seven-thirty. Date fell through.

She pressed send and took a cleansing breath in and then out her nose. Things rarely worked out for Loser Girls. She had to accept it. She focused on her fanfic story. Spock's daughter was pulling double shifts on the water reclamation planet.

T'Pak wearily stirred the vat filters of the water tank one more time. She'd worked for three full days with no rest. Water reclamation was grueling work, and the smell was awful. As she looked through the grating to the chambers of the privileged below, she saw a commanding figure. He strode across the floor, but suddenly stopped and looked up.

It was the Gorn prince.

T'pak gazed into Prince Vol's reptilian eyes. They shared a moment of such complex feeling and depth that it was beyond all language. It was a primal bond promising great passion. Souls destined to intertwine, a melding of two into one.

Elva carefully worked in the passionate tension for the coming climax with the hot prince.

The next day, Wyatt avoided her like the swine flu. It was hotter than h-e-double-hockey-sticks in the warehouse, but she kept doggedly clamping pipe. The thick scabbed blisters on her palms ached. After work, she was so beyond beat, she considered texting Margarett and telling her to not pick her up.

When they got back to the shop, Mr. Bob called Elva, Wyatt, and Yves into his office. Elva choked on a puff of smoke from Mr. Bob's Cuban cigar.

Wyatt thumped her shoulders.

"Your damn grandpa called a damn hour ago," Mr. Bob said. "He's caught in damn traffic near Conroe, dammit. He can't get back to the damn shop." He turned to Yves. "Damn Old Man Hicks needs us to drive her home."

"No way in hell," Yves said. "I told my wife I'd come straight home tonight. Wyatt, you have to do it."

"Hicks don't want Wyatt, but, damn, I can't do it either," Mr. Bob said.

"Wyatt, can you get her home on that bike?" Yves asked.

"I don't have an extra helmet," Wyatt said.

No one spoke to Elva. She had the same scintillating presence as the vomit-colored shag carpet covering the office floor. She didn't know if she wanted to go with Wyatt. On the one hand,was the Wyatt of kisses, on the other was Wyatt, the ass.

"Damn, don't tell Old Man Hicks I had you take her." Mr. Bob said, turning to Wyatt. "One of my grandson's damn helmets is in my Caddy that the damn gal can use."

Mr. Bob gave Wyatt a twenty.

Wyatt slipped it into his wallet. "All right."

Elva wanted to protest, but Wyatt was the only choice. She had to accept it, dang it.

Mr. Bob fetched the helmet and gave Wyatt a stern stare.

"Bring the damn helmet back on Monday."

Elva cast Wyatt a sideways glance. He wasn't happy. No not one bit. She followed him out to his Harley. They stopped beside it, and he placed a hand on her shoulder.

"I'm sorry about picking on you yesterday. I can't risk landing on the wrong side of Mr. Bob. You can understand that." He chucked her under the chin with a knuckle.

Elva nodded her head, though in truth she

didn't understand at all.

"You ever been on a motorcycle?" Wyatt asked. His voice was almost kind.

"No." She'd never done it, so why lie?

"Are you scared?" Wyatt asked.

"Hell, no." Elva snapped on the helmet. She eyed the powerful machine and ran a hand over the handlebar.

Wyatt didn't understand that 'to boldly go where no one had gone before' was part of the double helix forming her DNA.

16 COSMO GODDESS

"Swing your leg over the seat, Elva," Wyatt said.

She tried not to moan as she stepped over the bike. Could your leg break off from soreness? Could you dissolve at the same time because of excitement? Wyatt gave her a piercing stare as she settled on the creaking black leather. She stared right back, letting her soul shine in her eyes. It felt like a deep spiritual connection.

REAL.

He swung on the bike in front of her and kick-started the engine. Her helmet muffled the roaring, but she couldn't ignore the reverberations in her heart. Elva grabbed hold of the back of the seat and tried not to notice every one of her inner thigh molecules rubbing down Wyatt's backside. A hot hum snaked through her stomach and even lower.

Wyatt shouted something at her.

"What?" Elva tapped the helmet. He reached behind, firmly planting her hands on his waist, and then gunned out of the parking lot.

They pulled onto the freeway, weaving in and out between the cars. She leaned against him and enjoyed the ride. A simple conversation was all they needed. She and Wyatt had genuine chemistry. She'd read him wrong. She'd ask him to the pancake supper at her house. Her stomach was flopping with excitement when Wyatt exited the freeway at the Galleria and entered a parking lot.

Oh my, she thought, Wyatt was stopping to apologize for his crass remarks the day before. He had to be. Elva felt it in her bones. He guided the bike through the lot and rolled to a stop in front of Lord and Taylor.

A funny place to talk.

A tall, beautiful blond sauntered toward them. Her platinum hair swung and her designer jeans clung to her like they were painted on. Spiked high heels tapped on the concrete, and the girl's make-up brightened her cheeks and accented her eyes perfectly.

She was a *Cosmo* goddess.

Wyatt booted the kickstand, and Miss Absolutely Perfect leaned in for an open-mouthed kiss. A wave of floral-candy perfume gassed Elva to the point of asphyxiation. She pushed back on the seat, trying to scoot as far away as possible from the groping two. Wyatt's butt pushed against

Elva's thigh as the goddess sucked his face.

Fiery anger licked in Elva. Wyatt had some kind of freaking nerve. A book of revelations opened. He didn't know she was alive. She was sturdy, dependable, a hoot, sweet, maybe worth a roll in the hay, but she was never going to get a guy like him. Not ever. Access to Wyatt had never been in her Loser Girl's cards.

Elva shoved Wyatt hard, but she might as well have pushed against a brick wall.

Her move did grab the goddess's attention. "Wyatt, honey, what is this thing on the back of your bike?" The goddess pointed a meticulously done French-manicured nail at Elva, like this was a distasteful alien first contact situation.

"That's the plumber gal," Wyatt said. "Mr. Bob asked me to drive her home."

The goddess answered with wrath. "Hell, Wyatt, you said you were going to give me a ride home." She pulled away and placed a hand on her hip.

"Baby, I'm doing this as a favor for my boss. He handed me a twenty." Wyatt reached in his back pocket. His fingers brushed Elva's inner thigh. She tasted vomit in her mouth. "Go in the mall and buy yourself something. I'll be back for you when I'm done."

"Let me off." Elva pushed Wyatt again, but he ignored her. At the same time, the goddess plucked the wallet from his fingers and pulled out his cash. He and the goddess shared another lingering kiss, and Elva tried to squirm off the bike, but couldn't manage it unless Wyatt moved his skinny butt. This was like being forced to watch the series finale of *Enterprise* over and over forever. Why didn't transporters exist? They would be oh so helpful. Lifesaving. "Later, baby." Wyatt gasped for air, breaking the kiss.

"Don't take too long." The goddess adjusted her tank top. "I'll be waiting." She licked her upper lip and sauntered away with platinum blond hair swinging.

Plumber gal. A need to laugh hysterically almost unbalanced Elva. When Wyatt had kissed her in the truck, he hadn't seen her, known her. He was wrapped up in mindless lust. Humiliation coming to a Loser Girl wasn't right.

No, no, no.

"Let's get you home," Wyatt said, snapping the strap on his helmet.

Elva placed her hands around Wyatt's muscled waist. Her life was worse than God Awful Fanfic. Why hadn't she connected the dots—*GQ* god to *Cosmo* goddess? Oh, the humanity! Elva endured the ride home with stoic calmness cultivated by years of high school abuse. Heat blasted off the dingy freeway and masses of bugs smashed against her.

When they crossed the old bridge that led to her house, they were both surprised by a large barn owl standing in the road. It flew off as Wyatt pulled the bike up to the house. Elva knew the owl was a sign that she'd come into real wisdom about the unfairness of life.

"Is that you, Elva Presley?" Nonny stepped out on the front porch. "Margarett and her boyfriend came by earlier. They said they'd be back soon to pick you up."

"Bye, Wyatt." Elva scrambled off the bike and tossed her helmet at him. He left without even a nod for Nonny. She was done with Wyatt.

She rushed to her room and dove onto her bed, smashed bug goo and all. Why did everything have to hurt so much? Was she broken on a genetic level? Had a killer virus infected her with bad luck with guys? She needed her mom right now.

Willa Jo would be only thirty-three. She'd be married to a millionaire and work in a fancy office in downtown Houston. They'd live in a McMansion in classy Bellaire, and Elva'd have a brand-spanking new Mini Cooper. And most of all she'd have a mom. Elva longed to talk to her mother, to hug her, and hear her whisper everything would be all right.

But the flood waters had taken out that bridge long ago. Elva didn't even have a tombstone to visit—Willa Jo's ashes had been scattered in the Gulf.

"Elva Presley, did that man do something untoward to you?" Nonny stood at her door. Her words were clipped, no nonsense.

"No, Nonny," Elva said. "He just gave me a ride home."

Nonny paused. "You know you can tell me

anything."

"Nothing happened." Elva brushed at the oozing bug goo on her Dickies. "I'm taking a bath."

Minutes later she sank into a tub of steaming water, uncomfortably aware that her boobs were protruding above the water level. She'd been a double D-cup since the seventh grade, earning her plenty of unwanted attention from boys, never the tender attraction she longed for.

She lay until a trickle of honesty began to spread into her. She'd never been that into Wyatt. She liked the packaging, but not him really.

She inventoried her upsides: her flawless skin, her sea-colored eyes, and her endless gumption. The Wyatt incident had stirred hope for things. Hope was dangerous and could lead to Twinkies, bowls of Captain Crunch, and even more giant pants. Loser girls found guys in humongous fat guy shorts, who lived with their mothers and played online games 24/7.

But she wanted more, even if Wyatt wasn't the answer.

The basic hidden thing that every Loser Girl knows—she has value, like every person, star, whale, rock, and slug.

The whole universe has its share of risks. Slugs get stepped on, whales are hunted, stars explode, and people, well, people are fragile, easy to break. She was a secret unseen commodity, like di-lithium crystals found on planets that few would visit and even fewer could endure. Riches hid inside of her.

No one had found them yet. But they would.

It was just how the universe was put together.

The best part—this last thought sank into her like a spa treatment—she had potential. *Cosmo*-goddesses had nowhere to go but down. Elva had mountains to climb and stars to reach for. She had a job with cold, hard, yet liberating cash.

Amen.

17 PANCAKE SUPPER

Elva was turning prune-y when Nonny called, "Margarett's here!"

She climbed out of the bathtub and pulled on her clothes. Part of her wanted to stay home and eat an entire box of Twinkies, but she wasn't going to do that. She put a smile on her face and prepared to have a good time. At least that's what she told herself.

Margarett climbed in her bedroom through the window. Her mousey hair swung loose all the way down to her butt. Her canary yellow polyester jumper had been replaced with blue jeans and a baby doll-T.

"What in the heck happened to you?" Elva asked.

Not in all of Elva's years of knowing Margarett

had she seen her out of her signature jumper and coordinating bun. Stylish clothes made Margarett better than normal, cute. She peered at Margarett's face. "Are you wearing makeup?"

Margarett blushed. "Chase bought me Kohl eyeliner. He says the smoky purple brings out the lights in my eyes."

And it did.

An arrow of envy stabbed Elva's heart. Margarett was on cloud nine, while Elva was earth-bound. The Wyatt incident fallout pricked at her. How could the Universe fix things for Margarett and leave her out in the cold? She fumbled for her juicy magenta nail polish on the nightstand and hid her pain-stricken face from Margarett. It would make everything worse to be pitied.

"Time for the Eleventh Annual Pancake Supper. Let's go support the food bank!" Margarett said, bouncing once and then sitting on the bed.

"Don't rush me."

"That Wyatt boy didn't work out, did he?" Margarett asked.

"No." Elva rubbed away a detested tear.

"I'm sorry," Margarett said. "But come anyway. One stupid boy shouldn't stop your life. Pancakes will cheer you up."

"You're right." Elva straightened her rounded shoulders. She had to rise up or Margarett might keep giving advice. She dug her flip-flops out of the laundry basket.

"Shay's meeting us there after work, and you can

bring the fanfic." Margarett smiled.

"OK, OK, I'm going." Elva bunched her hair into a scrunchie. "But you need to know, all this perkiness is creeping me out."

"Oh, Elva, it's me." Margarett laughed. "I've still got the Holy Spirit. Don't worry."

Elva laughed too. Despite everything it felt good to hang out with Margarett. She tucked the copy of her fanfic in her backpack. Working on it might help center her being.

"We're going to have so much fun!" Margarett practically dragged Elva outside to Chase Fleaso waiting in the truck.

"Chase is so nice to drive us," Margarett said. "He bought me these jeans, too. Chase says my hair is beautiful long, and that's why I've got it loose. He thinks I ought to get it cut."

"By all means, do everything exactly the way Chase wants it." Elva recognized Margarett's improvements, but couldn't hold down the bite of jealousy. The pink-skinned pig farmer was way more than she'd thought. Margarett with real clothes and make up, what would be next? Elva remembered the day she'd considered Chase. Perhaps she shouldn't have brushed him off. He'd given her her first kiss, and now had practically reinvented Margarett; he was panning out to be a catch.

Sort of.

A squishy noise came from Chase's chub as Margarett settled in next to him. Elva squirmed away from them. All that pudgy pink.

"Hey, Elva," Chase said.

"Hey." Elva lifted a hand in a half-hearted wave. In the twilight, she could see the sunny look on Margarett's face. Chase whistled as he drove to town. Elva didn't think she'd ever seen Margarett so happy, and truthfully she was glad Margarett was hanging on to Chase, glad that she was getting a happy slice in the pie of life; she deserved one.

Elva caught a glimpse of herself in the side mirror. She could see puniness in her face—no boyfriend, no possibility of a boyfriend. Oh cruel, cruel fate. No happy slice for her.

The truck bumped over the railroad tracks and then turned into the Holiness parking lot, stopping under a stately pecan tree. The place was alive with lights and music. Elva smelled the piles of fragrant pancakes.

"I have to help in the kitchen," Margarett said, rubbing noses with Chase. "I'll see you later, Butterfinger."

One thing for certain, Elva never wanted to know why Margarett was calling him Butterfinger.

Chase helped Margarett out of the driver's side and lovingly tapped her behind as she headed into Holiness. He then hopped around the truck to Elva's door. Elva groaned. Leaving her alone with Chase Fleaso didn't seem like a good idea. They had a history, albeit short and pathetic, but history nonetheless. Was he a two-timing snake? Would he try to plant another catfish kiss on her lips? Would she stop him?

Chase opened her door and leaned into her. His fleshy palms brushed up her arms, making her shiver. Flitting moon shadows filtered through pecan leaves and lit his face, hiding his double chins. He didn't look half-bad at the moment. He leaned in closer. Elva's eyes drifted shut. Why not? One stolen kiss had the potential of cheering her up, and she wouldn't let it go any further than that. They'd never tell Margarett.

Where was the harm?

She froze. Dear Lord, had she been tainted by Wyatt's poison? How would she scrub such a low-life act off her karma? This kiss would be unfair to Chase and Margarett, and Chase might get the wrong idea—Elva knew she and Chase would never be a couple, an item, nothing. Using him was beneath her. She'd wait for something wonderful— the right guy and the right moment. It was a clean, pure dream that would be wiped away forever by a Chase hook-up.

"Margarett is one of my best friends." Elva pushed against Chase's chest, but he didn't move a centimeter.

"I know," he answered, and his moist lips connected with her cheek. "I just wanted to thank you for turning me down. I'd have never come to know Margarett if you hadn't."

Elva's eyes widened at the choke in his voice. His eyes were swimming with tears.

"Are you OK, Chase?" she asked.

"I love her," he said and threw back his arms. "Love her! I love beautiful Margarett." He almost looked handsome.

Needless to say, Elva helped herself to three tall stacks of pancakes—fifteen in all.

She was stuffed when Shay moseyed in with Bobby Ray.

"Hey, Elva, where's the hottie you've been hinting about for days?" Shay smiled as Bobby Ray sat on one of the folding chairs. Shay joined him by straddling his knee.

"Wyatt didn't work out for Elva," Margarett said.

"I still have prospects," Elva said.

"I didn't say you didn't," Shay said.

"Of course you do." Margarett added.

Ouch, Margarett smoothing out things for her? Were they in a mirror universe? Elva was the leader of the Loser Girls, and it was time to get back on track.

"Let's play dominos." Elva dumped out the box of tiles on the table.

They played Texas 42 until midnight, and somewhere in the middle of a nail-biting game, a pure feeling of happy contentment settled over her.

It surprised her.

Life wasn't just about the big picture or the drama, it was just as much about precious moments strung together like turquoise beads on a string. For all the trouble and disaster that seemed to dog her path, she managed to love her life. She liked who she was becoming. Good things would follow.

She put down her double fives and won another game. Her knuckles rapped the wooden table for luck.

They played all evening and her fanfic remained untouched, but at the end, she had to admit she'd had a good time.

18 DIGGING

The next day was Sunday and Elva stared at the stars out her window. The morning glow hadn't touched the east horizon yet. She'd only had a couple hours of sleep. The good time feeling of the pancake supper had dissipated and her stomach ached; instead of happy thoughts, she detoured into "no boyfriend" misery.

Dang Wyatt.

Elva tossed her covers on the floor. Would her life ever take a serious turn for the better? Vibrations of bleakness rumbled through her. She slapped the bed. Maybe she couldn't fix the big picture, but she could be in charge of right now.

She climbed out of bed, dressed for work, and fed the goats. On the way to join Papaw in the truck, she grabbed her backpack with the printed draft of her fanfic. One step at a time, one thing after another, and her heavy thoughts dissipated like morning clouds scattering from the sun. Everything would be OK.

Then the phasers fired.

"I hope you're not getting too attached to those goats," Papaw said. "Nonny's got a buyer who's coming next week."

What!

Elva's heart beat violently. How could the goats be done? She swiped at swift acid tears on her cheeks. She felt like two cents. Worse, worthless. The goats were walking hunks of meat. Destiny seemed determined to take them down. Why wasn't the Universe being affected by all her positive efforts?

No use arguing with Papaw, treating goats like brethren was beyond him like space flight was beyond the Neanderthals. Nothing could open his eyes. She had to save the goats on her own.

But how?

She crossed her legs, tucking her feet under her and resting her hands on her knees. She gently brought together her thumbs and forefingers in a yoga mudra. Touching her thumb, the symbol of fire, to her forefinger, the symbol of air, was supposed to bring her sharp awareness—more *Wiki* research.

Breathe in and then out. Calm the mind. Focus.

Ideas began to flow.

Maybe Chase would have room for goats on his

pig farm. She'd have to ask Margarett.

The SPCA stopped cruelty to animals. They might help.

Weren't rescuers out there for animals? She'd call them all and find someone to take the goats in. Somebody would step up.

Speed bumps jarred her out of her meditation. Papaw pulled into the Whataburger. She looked up to see light glimmering in the east. A sliver of blinding sun rose at the horizon. A sure sign she was on the right track.

"You want the usual?" Papaw asked.

"With jalapenos." Elva dropped her legs to the floorboard and stretched.

She was crumpling up a hamburger wrapper when they reached the shop. Mr. Bob stood by the warehouse and spit on the pavement. He was already calling out the job assignments. Elva was about to stumble toward Yves and Wyatt—she couldn't bear to look at him. Why had she ever thought that he liked her? How could she have been so ignorant?

Then Mr. Bob's words brought her a big surprise. "Hicks, you're going with the Old Man's residential crew today."

Elva was on the digging crew with Papaw.

"Are you sure she can dig?" Mr. Bob asked her grandfather.

"Sure can. I'm sturdy," Elva answered and then returned to Papaw's truck. She'd miss her daily dose of second-hand pot but she wouldn't miss

Wyatt. No sir. Her nerves keyed down, and she clicked on her seatbelt. Except for worried thoughts about the goats she was just fine.

The drive to the jobsite took over an hour. She dozed off and would have slept the whole trip but was jolted awake when Papaw got into slowing traffic and cussed out every driver on Interstate 45. Elva sighed and pulled out her manuscript. She scanned through a few pages for errors. The story had to be perfect. She planned to post links on all the best forums. The whole world would read it. Her life would change forever.

She turned back to the pages and soon was immersed in the conflict between Spock and T'Pak.

"Was I a love child?" T'Pak asked.

"I am Vulcan," Spock replied. "You were illogical."

T'Pak's heart was breaking. Her own father didn't even care that she was alive.

Elva's writing so engrossed her, she didn't notice when they left the freeway and entered the new construction area of a subdivision.

"We're here," Papaw said.

Elva put her manuscript away and looked around. Thirty upscale houses in various states of development surrounded a small man-made lake.

"Such nice houses for septic systems," Papaw said, as he stopped the truck in front of a giant brown one with white trim and a porch bigger than their whole house. He reached for a set of plans behind the seat and started studying the layout of the job.

"I want you to take this key and walk up the road to that small trailer." Papaw didn't look away from the plans. "You'll find a couple dozen shovels. Lug them to the back of the house. Don't forget the sharpshooters."

"Why don't you use the backhoe?" Elva gestured at the large yellow machine on an empty lot down the road.

"We have to hand-dig this septic because of a natural gas pipeline." Papaw tossed her a key. "Now, go haul those shovels."

It took a half hour. She'd dumped the last of the long narrow shovels called sharpshooters on the pile by the house when a white box van pulled up. A roll-top door flipped up and a crowd of men climbed out.

"We're using illegals for this job and you," Papaw said. "Now you're going to find out what real plumbing is about." He handed Elva a shovel. "You'll be tossing loose dirt today."

The men conversed in Spanish but stopped short when they saw her. Then, they began to speak lightning-fast and pointed at her, laughing. One smacked several of the others, and they stopped teasing. Elva leaned on her shovel, waiting. It had been years since a taunt or a pointed finger had moved her. The hell of high school had made her immune to random teasing. Elva turned away from the men and faced the morning sun, taking a moment to feel its warmth.

She depended on the sun. Her kinship with the faithful yellow star was the truest thing ever. The sun may be insignificant if looked at according to the scheme of the vast universe, but in this corner of the Milky Way it was everything. All things were insignificant from certain points of view, but that wasn't the whole truth, not for the sun, not for her.

The men moved away as Papaw divided them into teams. Elva quietly waited for her shoveling assignment to begin and idly watched a huge black Bronco pull up. A tall boy, a little older than her, hopped out of it. She'd met him before, back at her first day on the job, at the Moore Plumbing Supply. His tawny eyes met hers with a surprised raised eyebrow.

She gave him a cool stare but inwardly surveyed the landscape—slim hips, too thin, wavy brown hair over his collar. He was no *GQ* hottie, but still okay. OK Guy. He clicked his key remote and the back hatch of the Bronco popped. She watched as he hefted a large tool box, put a roll of electrical cord over his shoulder and headed into the house. She noted his muscled forearms and the width of his shoulders.

"Elva, get over here and start digging," Papaw said. "Why in the hell aren't you listening?" He threw her a pair of worn leather gloves. Elva pulled them on, hopped in the trench, and began to scoop loose dirt out.

Hefting water jugs and drilling for a month had made her strong, and Elva didn't feel the burn of digging at first. About an hour later that burn had turned into a fire. Another hour later, she was struggling to stay upright as the muscles in her back cramped. She hobbled over to the water station and chugged a quart of water.

"Shit don't run uphill and payday is on Friday," she whispered, a new mantra she'd nabbed from Mr. Bob. Elva had to endure until noon, one more half-hour. She gripped the shovel and gritted her teeth, tossing dirt. Her churning stomach went unnoticed until she vomited.

"Stop."

She looked up.

"Enfermo. Sick."

One of the men, who shoveled further down the trench pointed at the house.

"In la casa, rest," said another man with a sharpshooter.

The trench seemed to spin. Rest sounded like an excellent idea. She wiped her face. Sweat drizzled down her neck, forming a muddy paste. Elva fetched another water bottle from the cooler and headed to the house. She had to take a break.

Inside the house, the sheetrock hadn't been hung. She sank down in the roughed-in laundry room, enjoying the coolness of the concrete slab.

"Are you all right?" The boy from the black Bronco squatted beside her. A chill raced down her spine at the vibrations of his raspy voice.

His coffee hair was backlit by the utility room window. It reminded her of a rock star at a concert.

"I'm hot, but still breathing," Elva mumbled. The room spun and her stomach ached with nausea.

The guy hooked his measuring tape to his belt.

"How many fingers am I holding up?" he asked.

"Two." Elva swatted at his hand. "I'm fine." She took another swig of her bottle, but then she gagged and threw up on the boy's fine steel-toed boots.

Not again!

Elva scooted away in mortification and he chuckled. Chuckled!

Was there no end to bad Loser Girl karma?

He rinsed off his shoes with a water bottle hooked to his belt. Then he took a drink and handed the bottle to Elva.

"Take a mouthful of water, swish it around and spit," he said, squatting next to her again.

Elva took the bottle and did as told.

"Rest until you feel better," he said "And drink plenty of water, but small sips only. Here's a mint to cut the bad taste."

He placed a plastic-wrapped red and white peppermint in her hand. Their fingers touched. An unexpected feeling shot down her spine and reached her toes in a split second. She wasn't sure what the feeling meant, but it was interesting.

"Uh, thank you." Elva met his eyes. The warmth of his body invaded her space.

He didn't speak but smiled. She saw his dimples

and all the crinkles around his eyes, and knew she'd never forget one crease on his face. He took an odd sort of breath and let it out quickly. His breath warmed her cheek and curled into her mouth. This was powerful good karma. He touched her shoulder, gentle, tentative. Elva touched the back of his hand. Both touches were lighter than a feather, but Elva experienced more from those touches than if she were in a hot passionate embrace like in one of Nonny's Harlequin novels.

Something psychic and deep, beyond all words, filled the space between them. Elva looked straight into his eyes. All the dizziness and weakness left her. He gazed back. She prized such an intimate moment with a total stranger. A sense of relief infused her. She wasn't destined to be alone. An untamed future beyond her imagining might be around the corner.

The boy pulled back on his haunches. Elva dropped her hand and pressed it to her heart.

"Later," he said and moved into the next room with his measuring tape. Elva closed her eyes and leaned back her head.

Later.

She didn't even know his name.

The moment nettled her. What had just happened? She closed her eyes and breathed slowly until her racing heart returned to normal.

After resting, she felt energized again and headed back to the trench. She popped the peppermint in her mouth, and the hot sweet taste cut the sour tang of vomit. Smiling, she picked up the shovel and started to toss the rich brown earth out of the septic line trench.

Her intentions were good, but the work had whittled her strength. A few hot tears of relief coursed down her cheeks when Papaw called, "Lunch time!"

Elva hobbled toward his truck. A smoldering pain knifed her knees. Digging. She tossed her gloves on the floor of the truck and looked around for OK Guy's Bronco but it was gone. Papaw joined her and turned on the engine. A blast of hot air burst out of a vent, startling her.

"I know a barbeque joint down the road," Papaw said.

She grunted but didn't answer. The effort of speaking was currently beyond her. The muscles in her shoulders and the backs of her legs continued to vibrate. She'd heard this was a symptom of extreme physical exercise. She'd never felt anything like it before. "Fascinating," that's what Spock would say.

"Do you want to come with?" Papaw asked, as he pulled up to the Big Ole Texas Bar-b-que. The shack by the side of the road was surrounded with rickety picnic tables and pick-ups.

"I'll wait here," Elva said. "Will you leave the truck running?"

"OK, but watch the engine light. If it turns on, the air conditioning goes off." Papaw stepped out of the truck. "Do you want to try cabrito?"

Cabrito, like she'd ever eat goat.

"I'll have the chicken, a sour pickle, a slice of cheddar and white bread. No beans," Elva said. She had to cut back on the calories somewhere. "I'd like about a gallon of Coke though."

Papaw went into the shack, and she pressed her face onto the vent, letting the ice cold air conditioning freeze her cheeks. She pulled out her phone and texted Margarett.

Margarett, can you ask Chase if his family can take my goats?

When Papaw came with the barbeque, she caught a glimpse of herself in the side view mirror. The shape of the air conditioning vent was imprinted on her cheek.

After lunch, Elva shoveled until the sun cast long shadows. Digging washed the strength out of her like a flash flood cleared out a gully.

19 KEEP DIGGING

For the next few days she kept digging. It stripped her to the bare bones of existence. She couldn't think about Wyatt, she couldn't think about anything. The heat, the work, food, sleep, everything blurred together; she even dreamed about digging. She was so drained she didn't work on saving the goats. Only one hope smoldered, the chance to see OK Guy's Bronco at the jobsite again, but nada, he didn't show.

On Thursday, Elva put away the shovels and dragged herself to the truck. All her joints made creaking sounds.

"You're doing good work, gal," Papaw said as she climbed in.

"Uh huh." Elva grunted. She fell asleep before he pulled out of the subdivision. At home, Nonny had dinner ready. Elva's eyelids sank like lead sinkers as she tried to eat. The next thing she knew Margarett was shaking her shoulder.

"Elva, wake up."

Elva stretched. An untouched plate of macaroni and cheese dotted with hotdog slices sat next to a pool of her drool. She mopped it up with a paper napkin and noted Margarett wore blue jeans, t-shirt and her Wal-Mart vest. Whoa, Margarett was dressing normal 24/7.

"Did you feed the kids this afternoon?" Elva rubbed the back of her head, trying to clear the cobwebs.

"I had a long shift," Margarett said. "So, no. By the way, Chase told me he can't take those goats. He said the folks up at the Belling Meat Market will give you $100 apiece if they weigh over fifty pounds." She began to empty the clean dishes out of the sink.

Elva rubbed her temples with two fingers. Goat rescue was so much easier said than done, and she was quickly running out of options. Papaw snored in front of the TV.

Where was Nonny?

Speak of the devil.

"Good to see you up." Nonny yawned as she entered the kitchen. Her grandmother was dressed in the same snap-up-the-front housecoat that she'd been wearing for the past three days. Her hair was unwashed and tangled.

"Nonny, have you been taking your Zoloft?"

Elva asked.

Nonny's lip trembled. "It's been hit or miss."

"If you don't take it every day for at least a few weeks, it ain't going to help."

"It's hard to change."

"Anybody can change. Look at Margarett." Elva shook her fork at Margarett's blue jeans. "She's wearing denim."

"Miz Hicks, it's true. Jesus will help you change." Margarett squirted soap into the sink.

"There you go," Elva said. "Margarett's out of the glue that's been holding her down her whole life. She's tossed out her ugly old jumpers, and she isn't wearing giant buns anymore. Her weirdness is the past. Isn't that right Margarett?"

Margarett didn't answer. Her fair skin suddenly turned an odd purple color. She smacked down the bottle of liquid soap, and a stack of plates clattered in the sink. Even the collection of blue glass bottles in the kitchen window clinked together from the force of the blow.

"Margarett?" Elva asked.

"What … do … you mean … ugly jumpers and weirdness … ?" Margarett stammered.

"I mean your whole new life because of Chase. It's totally normal."

"That is so mean!" Margarett said. "I've always been normal. Always!"

"I don't think Elva Presley meant what you're thinking," Nonny said.

"I do mean what I said!" Elva pushed up from

the table.

"Take it back." Margarett turned off the water and crossed her arms.

"I meant every word of it." Elva did, and she couldn't believe the way Margarett was acting.

"If I wanted to live with poisonous snakes, I could've stayed at home," Margarett said.

"Don't be silly. You can't go home to your parents." Elva lifted her plate and forked up another bite of cold hotdog mac. "They'll ruin all your good changes with all their Holy Ghost nonsense."

"I'm not silly!" Margarett said. "And neither is the Holy Ghost. My parents love me, and they want me to come home. Mama even came by work today. Maybe I should just go." Margarett randomly squirted more soap into a pot.

"Girls, don't fight. You're friends." Nonny poured some Doritos into a bowl. "And it's almost that time of the month."

"I'll let it go if she will," Margarett said.

"Not happening. Your home messed you up. That's just the truth." Elva crossed her arms.

"That's it, Elva! I'm calling Chase to come and get me right now." Margarett threw a sponge into the sink and ran toward the bedroom. Elva winced when she saw the tears streaming down Margarett's face.

"Elva Presley, you need to apologize." Nonny spooned the last of the hotdog mac next to her Doritos.

"Don't tell me what to do, Nonny. You need to take your Zoloft and get a life."

Elva placed her unfinished plate in the sink. Her appetite had disappeared. Nonny took over the living room, and Margarett holed up in the bedroom. Elva locked herself in the bathroom. She turned on the water as hot as she could stand. Her muscles still throbbed, so she soaked in the tub until a few of the kinks let loose. After, she found Margarett, still sulking.

"Could you go away until I leave?" Margarett hissed. Her laundry basket was half-packed.

Elva had never seen Margarett this angry ever. Nonny was still watching TV, and ignored her. Fine. Elva sprayed herself with Deep Woods Off and tucked her yoga mat under her arm. Warm night air slid over her skin. She stopped under the Mimosa tree in the backyard and bowed to the bright moon overhead. A cacophony of croaking tree frogs and chirring katydids welled around her.

She rolled out her mat and then folded into downward facing dog, stretching one leg and then the other. It was a waste of time to be angry at Nonny or Margarett. They were caught in fearsome winds.

Elva's chest expanded as she drew in a deep breath and rose to standing. She tucked her foot up on her thigh, moving into a perfect tree pose. She let the pose fill her. She was a sturdy live oak. The windstorms of life had twisted Margarett into an impossible shape; they had broken Nonny into pieces. But the windstorms had brought something precious to Elva—something she treasured. Every breath she'd ever taken.

The Universe had a reason for all things.

Elva moved through a set of yoga poses, ending with a bow in a sweeping flow to the shining moon. Her grapefruit-sized breasts squished to her knees and she noticed they had shrunk a bit, and her legs were trimmer than a week ago. She sank to the ground in a grateful child's pose, but her head jerked up at the sound of singing.

"*Send thine angels now to carry me to realms of endless day.*" Nonny's reedy voice crooned an old hymn from the breezeway.

Elva rolled up her mat and peeked inside. Nonny had changed her housecoat and brushed her hair. She was feeding the goats.

Elva folded her hands and bowed in secret just outside.

Namaste. To you, Nonny, for trying. To you.

In her room, Elva found Margarett dressed in the old canary yellow jumper. Her hair was back in a long braid, and her packed laundry basket was in her lap.

"Daddy's coming to get me," Margarett said.

"Oh, Margarett." Elva dropped on the bed beside her. "Don't go. I'm sorry."

"I have to." Margarett shifted the laundry basket. "It's time. I need to get right with God. I have to start by honoring my parents."

The stupid Pentecostal glue. Elva bit her lower

lip. It was the dang stickiest stuff in the universe.

When Margarett left, Elva wanted to kick herself. She should have watched her words. Would Margarett's good changes unravel because of her? The awful feeling kept her awake. Elva tried to call Margarett, but the ring sounded from a pile of clothes on the floor. Margarett had left her phone behind.

It figured. A cell phone was the mark of the beast to Margarett's dad.

Elva texted Shay.

Margarett 911, call me!

But Shay didn't respond. Elva strangely wished Nonny hadn't taken care of the goats. They would have given her something to do. Then she remembered her fanfic. She hopped out of bed and waited as her computer crunched slowly to life. When her file finally opened, her fingers set the keyboard clattering.

Brigitte put on the ancient cloak at the doorway of the temple.

"I can't live with you infidels any longer." Brigitte put a hand to her forehead. "Chopping meat for Gorns is not for me."

"I thought you could change," T'Pak said. "You've made connections here. You have a mating companion."

"My people have deep traditions," Brigitte said. "I must return to my collective."

T'Pak would never forget the opening of the rough temple doors and her friend walking inside. Brigitte belonged to an underdeveloped civilization—one that had centuries of evolution to go through before it would receive membership in the Federation.

"Think of me as you travel the galaxy," Brigitte said.

T'Pak raised her hand in the famous Vulcan salute. "Live long and prosper."

The doors of the temple closed. Brigitte disappeared, maybe forever.

Elva shuddered as she typed. The emotion she'd created transcended everything before. Her fanfic was coming together. Soon she'd load it to a fanfic website. The only obstacle was finding a time to post. She never got home early enough for the library. She needed reliable Internet access and a computer, then wham! Soon the whole Web would know how brilliant her *Star Trek* story really was.

Elva typed in a new title. *Providence's Innocent* wasn't catchy enough. She morphed it into *The Death Incident.*

Perfect.

Only a couple of sleep hours remained when Elva finally lost the wind in her fanfic sails. Waves of sleep crashed over her. She imagined hundreds, no millions of people surfing the web to her story as she entered freefall into dreamland.

The morning came faster than warp speed. She groaned when Papaw barked her awake. "Get your dang butt out of bed."

"I hurt everywhere." Elva reached for the painkillers.

"Someday you'll die," Papaw said.

Real comforting.

"What are we doing today?" Elva asked.

"More digging."

Elva pulled on her Dickies, and the ibuprofen bottle went in her pocket. She fed the kids, robotic-like. Her mission was to get the next thing done. When she went back in the house, she was surprised to find Nonny cooking scrambled eggs.

"Do you plan to look for a job today?" Elva asked, scarfing her breakfast.

"I'm not ready yet," Nonny said. "But soon."

"Keep taking your Zoloft." Elva squeezed her hand.

She was surprised by Papaw's good mood when she climbed in the truck.

"Will wonders never cease," Papaw said, staring at Nonny waving at them from the window.

Nonny had made breakfast and seemed happy, and Papaw had let hope spring up. Elva wanted to believe that Nonny could stay on her medication and let go of the sadness that held her for so long, but one shaft of light wasn't enough to convince her that was finally happening.

They reached the jobsite mid-morning, and Elva spent another day shoveling dirt. She liked being outside where she could feel the breeze and listen to the cicadas. The worry of the goats, boy woes, and her friends slid away. She kept digging.

20 OK GUY

Back at it the next day, as Elva shoveled loose dirt out of the septic lines, she realized the Wyatt incident was fading.

How quickly the humiliation of passing first and second base with a loser dissipated like so much water spilt on hot pavement. Wyatt was a wound that would heal without any scars. Elva jammed her shovel deep into the soil. She could feel the muscles in her core flex. Digging was making her inwardly powerful and physically strong.

At lunchtime, Papaw brought in sack lunches for the whole crew—Antone's Famous Po' Boys. Pastrami, ham, bologna, and cheese on bread slathered with chow chow with a side of jalapeno chips and a Dr Pepper.

"Folks work harder with lunch," he said.

Elva agreed. She found a shaded place inside the roughed-in house to scarf her spicy-hot chips and crusty po'boy. She was noodle limp from the heat, but food sent a surge of energy down to her toes. When she was finished, she texted Shay again, but not even one response had showed up about the Margarett 911. It made sense though. What was Shay going to do?

Plenty of the lunch hour remained after eating, so Elva worked on goat salvation. She called a number she'd gotten from the SPCA; the place took in rescued farm animals. They didn't currently have space for goats, but they gave her a couple of more numbers to try. Unfortunately, both of them were disconnected. It was time to move to Plan B.

She called the guy buying the goats.

"Señor, this is Miz Hicks, I'm sorry to tell you the goats aren't for sale … I know you planned to pick them up tomorrow, but they are no longer available … Sí, sí, I'm sorry too."

And that was it. Bones, M'Benga, and Christine would keep on living for now.

The pleasure of goat reprieve sent a rush of creative power through her system, and she spent the last fifteen minutes of lunch working on fanfic. She brought out her manuscript and scribbled notes in the margins while sipping the last of her Dr Pepper. A hand touched her shoulder.

"How are you? The gravelly voice was dangerously close to her ear.

Cough. Cough. Gurgle. Dr Pepper splashed on

her shirt.

"Good." Elva caught her breath. OK Guy squatted next her, his legs wide apart. He wore shorts, and she suddenly felt shy.

"Sorry I scared you."

"I've been wondering what happened to you," she said. No. No. That wasn't what she meant to say.

A deep dimple indented his cheek, accenting a lopsided smile. The hardware was so easy on the eyes—nice biceps, wide shoulders, and his legs and arms were dusted with silky black hairs.

"Been busy. My name's Mitch by the way, Mitch McCall." He put out his hand.

Elva noted his neatly trimmed nails and his smell—sweat and plain soap.

"Nice to meet you." She wiped her hand on her Dickies and offered a firm handshake.

"Likewise." His short matter-of-fact answers communicated an odd form of Zen peace. "So, dove, what's your name?"

He was so close Elva could smell his cinnamon-ny breath.

"Elva Presley Hicks." She leaned back a bit. He was tall, even squatting. Mitch stared back with open curiosity.

"Really?" he asked.

She could read his sense of humor and open-hearted nature in his wide set eyes, but he didn't laugh at her name.

"Really," she answered. "My nonny named me.

She was trying to stir up good karma."

"Looks like it worked." His stare was beyond penetrating. They cosmically connected on an elemental level. It was like a mind meld, she felt so close to him.

"I've never seen a girl work like you. Good things are going to come to you." Mitch's voice gave her stacks of goose bumps. He settled down beside her cross-legged and his knee cap touched her thigh. Then, he took her hand. Oooh.

"You've got strong lines." He touched a crease across her palm. "See how your lifeline slants; you're destined for adventure."

"How do you know palm reading?" Elva asked.

"One of my dad's girlfriends was a psychic."

"Do you believe in it?"

"No, but I think that destiny is out there, and you can lay hold of it if you try hard." He ran his thumb over the thick callous on her palm. "I'd like to believe signs are everywhere even in the palm of your hand."

She tried to be cool, like a boy reading her palm was an everyday occurrence.

But she wasn't cool, she was on fire, and dang mad at herself, too. Hadn't she learned anything from the Wyatt incident? Opening up to someone left you exposed. Mitch could be a stalker or worse, and here she was jumping right back in the deep fat fryer. She should move therapy up on her list of things to do. She pulled back her hand.

He let it go but didn't move away. His eyes

drifted downward, landing on her *Star Trek* notes. She scooted the papers under her backpack. Papaw wasn't the only one who might not understand her love of *Star Trek*.

"What are you writing?" He reached for the curled edges of the sheets peeking out.

"You're kinda nosy." Elva stuffed the sheets in her pack and zipped it shut. She gave him a "get out of my space look."

Mitch didn't move an inch and neither did Elva. His gaze slid over her—her face, boobs, the curve of her waist and hips, down to her boots, and slowly back to her eyes. Was the air bristling with electricity? He tucked a stray strand of hair behind her ear and then traced the curve of her cheek with a knuckle.

"Let me see your phone."

"Why?"

"I'll put my number in it. I'm working, but we should talk later." He put up his hands. "Only if you want."

Elva reached in her pocket and handed him her phone. She had to boldly go.

He punched in his number and then pressed send. His phone rang, old school, like a bell. "I'll call you later."

"I might pick up." Elva said, and he winked.

Nice.

As he walked away, Elva fanned her face and thoroughly checked out his flat, tight, butt. *Very Nice.*

He drove away in his Bronco. This was a definite curve ball from the Universe.

"I'll call you later," he'd said.

The urge to connect with him was strong, but she didn't know if he was a Mega-lotto jackpot or a rip-off piece of junk from the Dollar Store. This possible relationship had a big red sign flashing over it: proceed with caution.

The cheery sound of the *Star Trek* theme from her phone brought her back to earth.

"Hello." Elva flipped open her cell. If it was Mitch, stalker weird-o, she was deleting his number right then.

"Elva, is that you?" It was Margarett. Elva hadn't heard from her since their fight. She must have stopped by the house for her phone.

"Oh, Margarett, thanks for calling." Elva breathed a deep sigh of relief. "I'm really sorry about our fight. My heart is in the right place. I didn't want you to mess stuff up with Chase. He's a great guy."

"No worries. I'm home again, and I wanted my best friend in the whole world to hear the news before it comes out in the *Belling Citizen*."

"What's that?" Elva asked.

"I'm getting married in August."

Elva didn't know what to say. Her options: 1. Are you incredibly, impossibly, unimaginably IGNORANT? 2. That's the most dumb-ox, impaired thing I've ever heard. 3. Why in the cussed hell would you do that?

Thankfully Margarett chattered on and didn't leave space for Elva to slide a word in edgewise.

"I'm engaged to Chase Fleaso," she squealed.

Elva tried to breathe through the horror. A part of her tribe, a friend of *Star Trek*, and a charter-member Loser Girl of the Universe, dear God, Margarett was getting married. Some things didn't need words. She had no clue how to help Margarett out of this mess.

"Elva, did you hear me? I'm getting married to Chase the second week of August at Holiness right before school starts!"

"Uh, that's interesting," Elva said.

Margarett gushed on. "I want you to be my bridesmaid."

"Er, OK … "

"You and Shay will be my bridesmaids. It has to be that way! Next Friday's the Fourth. We'll shop for my wedding dress and your bridesmaid dresses. You don't mind paying for your own dress, do you?" Margarett never took a breath. "After that we'll watch the fireworks from the roof of the Galleria." Her words slapped around like schooling minnows. Elva struggled to breathe, just breathe.

"I don't know," Elva said. "I'm buying my new computer over the Fourth and planning to post our fanfic story on the forums."

Margarett giggled. "Honey, I'm on the phone right now."

An answering growl that had to be Chase came

next. Elva struggled not to gag.

"Elva, you're *SO* funny talking about *Star Trek* fanfic." Margarett said. "But I'm serious. My wedding has to be perfect."

Elva certainly had not been joking about posting their story. Fanfic would keep them from being trapped in the tormenting darkness of small town Abaddon. How could that be silly? And anyway, who was acting like her gray matter was under an evil alien influence that caused rational thought to cease? Not the girl planning to post a *Star Trek* fanfic story.

"I'll see you on the Fourth," Margarett sang out merrily.

"Uh, OK," Elva muttered back. She shut the phone, leaned against the wall, and mouthed over and over—Margarett, Margarett, Margarett. She couldn't even say the name aloud because it was so painful.

Her cell rang again.

"Have you talked to her?" Shay asked.

"I just got off the phone."

"You were right about the Margarett 911," Shay said. "Now we have to go and buy bridesmaid dresses."

"Yeah, Friday, the Fourth," Elva answered and then they were both silent. She could hear Shay breathing.

"Monumental stupidity." Elva listened to phone static for half a minute more.

"No kidding." Shay finally spoke. "You need to

do something, Elva. Talk Margarett out of it."

"I know, but I don't know what to say," Elva said.

"You'll think of the right words," Shay said. "You always do. I'll see you on the Fourth." And she hung up.

Shay was right. She had to help Margarett see how crazy this wedding was. She had to. In the meantime, there was nothing to do. Loser Girls stuck together even if it was a plane wreck, even if it was a massive disaster like an oil spill, a hurricane, or a tsunami. She'd buy a bridesmaid dress and find a way to save Margarett. She would.

The next week Elva was trapped in a time-space anomaly called digging.

She hated digging.

She hated digging like Klingons hate Romulans.

She hated digging like tribbles hate Klingons and Romulans.

The day before the Fourth, Elva woke to Papaw's growl. "Elva, wake up!" She crawled out of bed like a feeble, old woman. She dreaded tomorrow's shopping trip for dresses.

Elva wrote during lunch and almost waltzed to the truck when Papaw surprised her by telling her to help pack up. They were going home early. She looked for Mitch but he hadn't showed. She opened her phone to check her calls. No calls from him. Not once. Let him call her first. She snoozed on the drive home. The truck jerked to a stop in traffic.

"Live long and prosper," Elva mumbled. A layer

of grit roughed her cheek that was smashed against the rolled up window.

"What in the hell did you say?" Papaw asked.

"I was dreaming about *Star Trek*."

"*Star Trek*." Papaw almost spat the words. "This is Nonny's doing. I can't believe my grown granddaughter's head is wrapped up in something so fool stupid."

Elva didn't answer. Papaw understood the Houston Texans, the Houston Astros, and Indy 500 stock car racing. Intelligent life existing out in the Universe was too much for him, way too much. She changed the subject. They dropped by the shop and picked up their pay. Cold hard cash forged a ceasefire between them.

"Ready to go to the bank?" Papaw asked.

"Absolutely."

Elva trembled as she deposited $1700 into her account for a total of almost seven thousand glorious dollars. The deposit slip put a warm glow inside her. Papaw had a list from Nonny so they stopped by the Dollar Store to shop. Elva bought a bag of nail polish with the colors of her dreams, including Tutu Mango, Trust Fund Baby Blue, and Saucy Chocolate. She found some clothes too— shorts that looked like an American flag, a sparkly t-shirt, and flip-flops with shiny bows. She was ready for the trip to the bridal store in the morning.

At home, Nonny had taken care of the goats and cleaned the house. Elva's laundry was folded on her bed. Papaw hugged Nonny, and she laughed.

Elva couldn't remember the last time she'd heard Nonny laugh. A pinch of yeast-like happiness warmed her insides. The Zoloft was finally kicking in. It was a real gift.

"Payday ought to mean something, darlin'." Papaw kissed Nonny. "Let's drive into Houston for your favorite Mexican food.

"Elva Presley, will you be all right alone?" Nonny asked.

"Honestly." Elva hated Mexican food. "I'll make mac and cheese."

Elva spent time with the kids before fixing her dinner. Christine, M'Benga, and Bones were getting so big. She opened the gate and let them run for a bit before sundown. They leaped on a propane tank behind the house. Without missing a step, they leaped off the tank and hurtled around the house. Around and around they went. Elva smiled at the frolicking babies. She didn't worry about them running off. The bottles of formula would reel them in.

She went in the house and began making their bottles. Nonny was primping in the bathroom.

"Glad you're taking good care of the goats." Papaw said. He'd shaved and smelled of Old Spice. "Nonny had another call about them. He's coming by to pick up the goats next Friday."

What! Elva nearly dropped a bottle on her toe.

"He's offering forty bucks for each one of them. That's some nice pocket change."

No! No!

172

A rogue wave of pain crushed Elva's chest. She tried to steady herself with a calming breath, but it didn't seem to work.

Cabrito. The goats were doomed roasts for a fiesta. Again.

She had to think fast.

"If we wait till they're bigger, the Belling Meat Market in town will pay a hundred apiece for them," Elva said. "We shouldn't take forty."

"Gal, don't talk nonsense," Papaw said. "Nobody will pay that much."

"Margarett's boyfriend said so. He said they need goats, but they have to be older with more meat. Do you want me to call them so you can talk to them?" Elva pulled out her cell phone.

"Naw, I'll call them later," Papaw said. "After I tell this new feller no." He smiled and winked at her.

Save. Inside she danced a happy dance. She'd given the goats more time.

Nonny and Papaw left for Houston and Mexican food, and Elva fed the goats.

"Y'all are safe for now. Elva placed her cheek next to M'Benga's warm body. His coat was losing its baby softness and had a more bristly texture. She could hear the powerful beat of his heart. Bones nuzzled her cheek. Christine leaped behind her, placing her delicate hooves on Elva's shoulder and then chewed on her hair.

"I'll figure out something." Elva hugged the goats. "I will."

21 FOURTH OF JULY

The Fourth was gorgeous. The sun shone, cardinals sang, and cicadas hummed, but Elva was spending the entire day shopping for a bridesmaid dress. Mucked-up Margarett was marrying Chase. Elva had no idea how to stop it. She toyed with the idea of telling Margarett she wouldn't be in the wedding, but she couldn't. Even though this was a strange new world no one needed to explore, Loser Girl loyalty pinned her. She couldn't abandon her friend. It was part of the deal. She had to talk Margarett out of this mess.

She tugged on her Dollar Store clothes, pleased that her new t-shirt was a mere 1x and only a touch tight, and the shorts were size 18! Down from size 22!

Elva peered into the cracked mirror in her closet

with the utmost satisfaction. In the kitchen, Nonny hummed. She stood at the stove, flipping flapjacks.

"Why are you so happy?" Elva took a stack of six and smeared each with real butter.

"I got a job," Nonny sat down with her own stack of flapjacks. "I'm working at the fireworks stand outside of town. Three hundred dollars for one day's work. How about that?"

"That's awesome, Nonny!" Elva smiled.

"It'll cover the back rent, and poor Uncle Sam, he ain't getting nothing."

"Good." Elva reached for the syrup and then stopped. She moved two cakes off the stack, back onto the serving plate.

Nonny copied Elva and pulled two cakes off her stack. "Never too late to start watching your weight."

Zoloft was a miracle drug. Most of time Elva couldn't see how she and Nonny were related, but when the black clouds rolled back, revealing Nonny's sunny side, Elva found a bit of herself in her grandmother. Under the sorrow and denial was a firecracker, full of sass. Elva's secret hope was Nonny would lose weight and finally get over Willa Jo's passing. If Nonny got set right, Papaw would follow. That's how things rolled with them. A few years on this side of heaven where she and her grandparents were happy and whole would mean something.

"I won't be back until late," Nonny said, finishing her flapjacks.

"Have fun," Elva answered. "I'm going out with Margarett and Shay."

"Fine, honey." Nonny loaded the glasses into the dishwasher and then stopped. "Elva Presley, I know you don't want those goats to die. You're a smart gal. Don't quit trying. You'll figure a way to save them."

Elva stared into her syrup swirls fully expecting to find a Virgin Mary.

Nonny left for work, and Elva waited in the yard for Margarett and Chase. She flipped open her cell phone to check for messages. Who was she kidding? She wanted to know if Mitch had called. He hadn't. There was a text from Margarett. Chase planned to drop them off for wedding shopping and the discount bridal store was cash only. Seven crisp twenties were tucked into Elva's back pocket, enough for the dress, lunch, and dinner. Shay planned to meet them at the store. After, they'd roam the mall, and then end the day watching fireworks from the roof of the Galleria.

Chase's pickup pulled up.

"Are you wearing those short shorts?" Margarett asked, opening the truck door. She was back in a denim jumper down to her ankles.

"I bought these special for the Fourth," Elva said.

Chase didn't say a word, but she caught the flick of his fleshy eyelid checking out her thighs.

He might love Margarett, but her thighs were worth a good long look.

The drive to Houston was tolerable. Margarett

flapped on about her wedding and the twelve children she and Chase planned to start having right away. Chase smacked gum, blowing an occasional bubble and popping it with a crack. Elva intermittently gave Margarett a sideways "what the hell" look, but her friend was floating on a puffy pink cloud of dream wedding happiness. Margarett kept squeezing Chase's arm as if checking to see if he was real. Elva couldn't help thinking she was watching one of those ill-fated stories like when McCoy and Kirk fell in love with that Nazi woman who had to die in the *Trek* classic "City on the Edge of Forever."

The truck thunked to a stop in front of Maria Magdalena's Bridal Warehouse.

"I'll be back in a couple of hours," Chase said.

Chase and Margarett shared a parting kiss and Elva cringed. She had to bring down this wedding. She had to. It was her job as the Loser Girl leader. She snorted in disgust and went in the bridal store. The puffy white dresses inside reminded her of Vidalia sweet onions. She inspected a particularly bulbous dress, and her eye began to twitch when she saw the price tag.

God help them.

Elva endured while Margarett tried on fourteen extremely cabbage-y dresses. Finally, Shay arrived with Bobby Ray in a red Sebring convertible. Elva saw them out the big picture window in the front of the store. Bobby Ray looked old in full sunlight, like he was thirty or more. He leaned over and kissed Shay full on the lips as she got out of the car. His hand reached out for an intimate groping squeeze of her butt. Double ewww.

Evil, evil, alien infestation was afoot. Elva imagined malignant worms resting at the base of her friends' skulls. These insidious intergalactic beings were bending Shay and Margarett to their nefarious wills.

Shay waltzed into the store. "Hey, gals!"

"What do you think about this dress?" Margarett asked.

"It's fabulous," Shay said, taking the chair next to Elva.

"It's, um, uh, white," Elva said. The dress was a giant taffeta bowl with sparkly beads and bloated sleeves.

"Of course it's white," Margarett said. "What do you think I am?"

"Don't you want to show your shoulders?" Shay asked.

"It wouldn't be seemly." Margarett swished the train around.

What the heck was seemly? What an ignorant way to spend the Fourth!

Elva was zipping up a banana yellow bridesmaid gown with six bunched rows of taffeta when the rousing sounds of the *Star Trek* theme filled the dressing room.

OK Guy had finally called.

"Hey, whatcha doing?" Mitch's voice was so freaking hot there needed to be a law against it.

"I'm with my friends. We're, um, trying on, um, clothes." Elva's voice was steady, but her heart skipped a beat or two.

Silence. Then Mitch said, "Oh."

"Yeah, my friend Margarett is getting married, and I just zipped on this banana yellow dress. I look like bloated cupcake."

"I doubt that," Mitch said.

It was nice of him to say. Real nice.

"So, why'd you call?" Elva asked.

"I was wondering if you were doing anything, but I guess you are."

Silence. Then Elva said, "Oh."

"What's taking so long?" Margarett rapped on the door of the changing room.

"I'll be out in a second. The zipper's caught." Elva spoke through the door and then whispered into the phone. "I can't get out of this shopping trip, but I'd really like to hang out with you. Can you call me later?"

"All right." Mitch's easy Texas twang vibrated right down into her core. "I'll call tomorrow, and we'll figure it out."

He hung up and Elva leaned against the wall. He was going to call again.

"Come on out." It was Shay this time. "You can't look any worse than me, like a fluffy school bus."

Elva didn't say anything about the phone call. Mitch had read her palm and called her on the phone, and that's all. Mitch news could wait until there was Mitch news.

Eventually, Elva was the proud owner of a bright pink bridesmaid gown, incrusted with sparkly sequins. Its full skirt made her hips look like the saucer section of the Enterprise, and her arms like the Enterprise's nacelles, the huge sausage-shaped engine thingies. At least the waist was snug.

Elva sighed as she handed over four twenties for the dress. Shay's dress was a slinky sheath the exact shade of pink as Elva's and five sizes smaller. Margarett's cabbage-y dress was white, with loose long sleeves and an ill-fitting bodice, but it was modest, by God, and that's what Margarett wanted.

A blast of hot air hit their faces as they stepped out of Magdalena's and piled into Chase's pickup for the drive to the Galleria. Elva's stomach rumbled. If she'd known they weren't eating lunch, she'd have eaten the extra pancakes at breakfast.

Chase bought them smoothies. Margarett didn't want to ice skate because she was wearing a dress and her unmentionables might show. Shay said her jeans were too tight for it. Elva just didn't want to ice skate. Chase spent an hour looking at knives in a hunting shop. Elva munched her way through an entire bag of kettle corn.

Finally they passed the Apple store. It was packed, but Elva wanted to talk to a sales person anyway.

"You can come back later," Shay said.

"But," Elva said.

"It's a big purchase." Shay interrupted. "Think

about it, and let's try on clothes."

Elva swallowed and nodded, following her friend away from the happy silver apples and sleek white cases.

Clothes shopping was beyond stupid. Elva noted that most of the stores didn't even carry her size, or, if they did, the plus-size selection was limited to gross hip-hugging jeans and skin tight t-shirts with cutesy sayings all over them. When Shay went into Victoria Secret to try on underwear, Elva headed back to the Apple store, but it had closed early for the Fourth.

She should have gone with Mitch.

Chase parked on the rooftop parking of the Galleria so they could watch the fireworks. At sunset, they met up at the truck. There weren't many people in this area waiting for the show. Chase and Margarett spent the time smooching in the cab of the truck, and Shay snoozed in back on a beach towel. For some reason Bobby Ray couldn't make the firework show.

Elva placed her lawn chair a discreet distance from the truck but she wasn't ready to sit. She turned her face toward the fading sunlight and lifted her hands high overhead. She stretched out to downward facing dog and then stepped forward for a lunge. Sweat poured off her face, and she slapped mosquitoes. Why hadn't she brought Off? At the end of sun salutation, she prayed she wouldn't catch West Nile Virus.

The fireworks shot off thirty minutes after

sunset, but most of the colorful bursts of light were half-hidden by a looming hotel.

They drove home and that was the "wrap" for the Fourth of July. Elva *wanted* to plumb the next day.

22 SETTING FIXTURES

Elva kept checking for a call from Mitch, but there was none the next day or the next. She decided not to call him back. Was it too much to ask for someone available? One phone call wasn't enough. She had Wyatt to thank for that bit of wisdom. Maybe she longed for the moon, and the stars, and the whole, dang universe, but deep inside a tiny voice whispered, she was worth it.

Digging hell went on for another week, and Elva chose to focus on one trouble at a time. She picked Margarett and texted her.

Margarett pick me up for church on Sunday evening.

As leader of the Loser Girls, intervention fell to her.

Margarett texted back.

Praise the Lord! Will be there at 5.

Elva readied herself for the coming encounter. On Saturday, she visited the library and researched teen marriage. Margarett arrived at five sharp, and Elva endured three hours of Holiness. The experience was similar to being trapped in the event horizon of a black hole where time stands still. Elva received two prophesies and had seven demons cast out before the preaching even started. Finally, during the spirit slaying, she was able to wheedle Margarett outside so they could talk.

A blue bug light cast an eerie hue on the porch.

"Margarett, I don't want you to take this the wrong way," Elva said.

"What are you talking about?" Margarett straightened her collar.

Elva plunged forward. "You shouldn't marry Chase right now. The Center for Disease Control says you have a fifty percent chance of being divorced. You gotta hear me. Marrying young leads to less! Less education. Less independence. Less experiences. You deserve more."

Margarett was quiet. Elva shuffled nervously, waiting for the tsunami of anger to hit, but Margarett didn't peep.

"Are you still speaking to me?" Elva asked.

Margarett faded into the blue shadows. Elva looked at her friend curiously.

"I hear you," Margarett finally said. "But I love Chase. He makes me a better person. I honestly believe we'll be that other fifty percent."

"You don't need him to be a better person," Elva

said. "Don't you want a better life? Don't you want him to have a better life?"

Margarett laughed. "Everybody can't be like you. You've known who you are since the seventh grade. I'm not like you. I'm never getting out this town. This place is what I know. This is what I am."

"You're still in high school." Elva didn't want tears to roll, but they did anyway. "Get your education first, a foundation you can build on. Be better."

Margarett sighed. "Elva, I love Chase, and he treats me good. I've got to get out of my house. You must understand that."

"I do. But there are choices—" Elva sputtered

Margarett put up a hand. "I've made up my mind. I hope you'll still come to my wedding."

Elva bit her bottom lip. Her research hadn't helped one bit. "Of course, I'll be there, but I wouldn't be a friend if I didn't tell you what I honestly think."

"I know you care." Margarett hugged her. "We better go back in the church."

"I'll wait in the truck," Elva said. "I only came so we could talk." She trudged back to the truck and sat on the open tailgate and swung her legs. Why did things always go the hard way? She stared up at the fathomless field of stars, baffled by one more mystery in the Universe.

***

The next day at the shop, Mr. Bob called out the assignments. "Hicks, you're with Yves."

Digging was over, and it was back with Yves, and, yes, Wyatt.

Yves smiled at Elva as she joined him by a white box van.

"What are we doing?" Elva asked.

"Setting fixtures. Water fountains, toilets, and urinals." Yves loaded extension cords into the back of the van. Wyatt slouched upfront in the driver's seat. A sharp jab of pain stabbed her when she saw him, but she shook it off.

He stuck his head out the window. "Gal, I can't believe you're still plumbing!"

He didn't even call her by name. Wyatt acted like his tongue hadn't ever licked around in her mouth, like he'd never squeezed her breast, like she'd never touched him. What had she ever seen in this clearly inferior life form?

"Let's go." Yves clapped his hands. "Hicks, Wyatt, y'all pick up the fixtures. Time's a wasting."

Elva nodded and climbed in the passenger side of the van. "Touch me again, and I'll tell my Papaw to fire your sorry butt." She snapped her fingers at Wyatt. "So what's today's plan?"

"Pick up the drinking fountains," Wyatt said, but his voice wobbled a touch. "And install them at the high school in Sugar Land. By the way, I hear you. Hands-off, but you'll never know what you're missing."

"As long as we're clear," Elva said.

Neither spoke another word on the way to the supply house. Wyatt backed up to the loading dock. He lit up a joint. The cab filled with tangy smoke.

"Load the fountains. I forgot to bring a dolly, so you'll have to make do." Wyatt pointed back at a row of large rectangular-shaped boxes waiting on the dock. "Get to it."

Elva pulled on her leather gloves and rolled off the high seat of the van. Heat already burned through the pavement into the soles of her shoes. She climbed on the dock and stretched her arms partway around one of the waiting boxes. It wasn't heavy, more dang awkward. She shoved her leg against it and slid it toward the van. The roll-top van door was closed. She reached for the small silver handle at the bottom. It sprung open and a hinge snapped, taking a small piece of her glove and bit of flesh with it.

"Gosh dang it all to hell!" Elva yapped like a coonhound. Blood spurted through the glove and she pressed her fingers against wound. It stung worse than a yellow jacket sting. Where was Wyatt? She craned her neck around the van and saw him in the side mirror. He took a deep drag on his joint.

She leaned against the row of boxes, cautiously letting go of the gash. Blood flowed, but it wasn't too bad. She balled up her hand into a fist to return pressure to it. With a shove, she went back to work. She loaded box after box. Sweat poured down her back. She slipped on the last one, wrenching her knee. Dang thing hurt more than her hand.

"You need help?" Yves asked, vaulting up next to her. His truck was parked beside the van. "What the hell happened to you?"

Elva glanced down. Her overalls' bib was stained with blood.

"Cut my hand," she said.

"Where's Wyatt?"

"Stoned out of his mind in the truck."

Yves grunted. "Let me see that cut."

Elva held out her hand. Blood had soaked her glove.

"I've got gauze and antibiotic gel in my truck. Go take care of it."

Elva was surprised by his show of humanity but was grateful. He jumped off the dock and beat on the cab.

"Wyatt, get the hell out of there."

Wyatt stumbled out of the van. "What do you want?"

"Don't ever smoke pot on the job again, or I'll fire your sorry ass. I don't want to see your face for the rest of this day. Get your butt out of here." Yves dug his heel into the blacktop.

"How am I getting home?" Wyatt slurred his words together.

"Call your girlfriend."

Yves was beyond a total hypocrite, and it pleased Elva to no end.

"Let's go, Elva." Yves said. "I'll send somebody

by to pick up my truck."

They left Wyatt and headed to Sugar Land. Elva carefully bandaged her hand as traffic snarled. Yves pulled into a Taco Bell. She was thankful she'd stuck an emergency ten in the top of her sock. She ordered two bean burritos, three crunchy tacos, and a Mountain Dew. The green fizzy soda nearly split her brain open with the cold rush. Hot sauce slopped on her palm causing it to throb again.

"You got any pain killers other than ibuprofen?" she asked. "My hand hurts."

"I've got pot," Yves said.

Elva wasn't quite ready to rack up misdemeanors.

"I'll pass."

At the high school, Yves cranked up crass rap music so loud that Elva felt vibrations in her heart. Yeah, it annoyed her, but she didn't say a word. Yves was her sort-of-hero today.

One by one they set the water fountains. They screwed metal plates into the walls, hung the boxy fountains, and connected a few pipes. Easy peasy.

Yves worked at a leisurely pace. "They don't pay us to work fast."

Elva nodded and didn't hurry; she wasn't even tired at the end of the day.

On the way home, they were caught in traffic. Elva's hand hurt too much for her to hold a pencil so tweaking *The Death Incident* was out. Poor Yves ran out of pot and cursed Wyatt every which way as they inched forward.

It was late when they got back to the shop, and Papaw was waiting.

"What did you do?" Papaw pointed at the blood stains on her shirt.

"Cut my hand." She lifted up her bandaged palm.

"You'll survive," he said.

Papaw hit the nail on the head. She was a survivor. Her life was about scraping by like a weed struggling in a sidewalk crack, but she wanted to do more than survive. Her want whispered in her bones.

They got home extra late, and Elva was starving. Nonny hadn't cooked dinner, and Elva would have complained, but Nonny had fed M'Benga, Christine, and Bones.

"What happened to your hand?" Nonny asked.

"I cut it." Elva said. "I'll survive."

"Why no dinner?" Papaw asked.

"It's two-for-one night at the Sonic Drive-in," Nonny said.

"Sounds good," Papaw rubbed his hands together. "Let's head over."

Elva changed into her faithful spandex jeans and enjoyed the pure satisfaction of them sagging around her thighs, instead of being skin tight, a giant leap toward plain normal.

At the Sonic, Papaw rolled down the window and ordered.

They were waiting for their food when Nonny pointed across the parking lot.

"Isn't that your friend Shay in that red Sebring?"

Elva sank down, peeping across the cars. Shay was kissing Bobby Ray, tobacco stained teeth and all. Oh, the humanity! What was wrong with Shay and were there any legal drugs that would fix it?

"I know that man's mama at the elementary," Nonny said. "I think he's married."

Elva dropped her head lower than the dashboard and thanked every lucky star over Texas that Shay hadn't looked their way. Informative words hovered on the tip of her tongue. *Don't come over, Shay,* Elva thought. *Don't even look my way, or I'll have to say something. These words might irreparably damage our friendship.*

Elva tried to stay put, but Bobby Ray was so less and she wanted to plunge his skinny butt in scalding water. Shay didn't have anyone to tell her the truth.

"Nonny, I'm going over to say hey to Shay."

"That's nice." Nonny said, and Elva tossed a pinch of salt over her shoulder for good luck. Her mission for the Loser Girls could not be ignored. She readied for battle and headed across the Sonic lot to where the Sebring was parked..

"Hey, Shay. Bobby Ray." She placed a hand on the shiny finish of his convertible.

Bobby Ray frowned. "Watch out for my car. It's special." His voice whined at a high pitch. Elva caught the look in his eyes. He was a coward. She was sure of it.

"Funny you should say that," Elva said. "I wish

you'd treat my friend as good as your car. But you don't, you lying skunk, and you know it. Karma's going to hunt you for messing with Shay."

"What are you talking about?" Shay pulled away from Bobby Ray. Her eyes blazed in anger.

"I'm sorry, but honesty is important." Elva stared at her friend with every bit of boldness she could muster. "Bobby Ray has something he needs to tell you about his marriage state. And he's way too old for you. You should dump his butt." Then she turned on Bobby Ray. Her eyes flared up like warp engines. "Everybody in town knows what you're doing. You're a freaking snake and should leave Shay before your ass ends up cooked."

Bobby Ray paled.

"What's gotten in to you, Elva?" Shay asked. "What kind of a friend are you?"

"A good one," Elva said.

"Gal, we've got your food," Papaw called.

Elva took a breath and looked at Bobby Ray and Shay's astonished faces, "Later then."

She returned to the pickup, hunkered down, and ate. When she'd polished off her double meat cheeseburger stacked with jalapenos, she checked to see if the Sebring was still there. It was gone.

23 HORROR

Back at the house, Elva hurried to the bathroom and turned on the water. Seeing Shay ripped around like that … she needed to be clean, very clean.

Elva soaked in hot-as-she-could-stand water to loosen embedded dirt on her elbows and knees. She pumped soap from an Elvis soap dispenser and scrubbed, careful not to take off her hide. The current status of the Loser Girls of the Universe wasn't a pretty picture. One Loser Girl was getting married to a pig farmer. The second was dating a 25-year-old loser. And Elva, number three, had no one. In the Loser Girls' universe, she had the best thing going. Dear Lord, she wanted to help her friends and herself, but she didn't have a clue how.

She pulled on her oversized sleep shirt and

climbed into bed. Her fanfic was at hand but she didn't touch it. Nothing was helping, not yoga, fanfic, or the goats. She was floating toward the abyss of nothing on a brimstone lake of a lesser life. Every night, she closed her eyes and the next thing she knew it was morning, and nothing changed. Was this all there was? As she drifted off, she wondered if lifting plumbing fixtures was worse than any form of torture used by the Romulans.

The following day began with goats and didn't seem like anything special. At least her hand was better. Elva was with Yves's crew again. Today, they were installing urinals at several sites. She loaded dozens of boxes into the van and then hauled the boxes out again to the jobsite. Wyatt and Yves did most of the installation, but she hung six urinals by herself.

The work went fast and it looked like they were going home early. After lunch, they had one more urinal for a residential site, a mammoth brick house in a McMansion neighborhood near Bellaire. The inside of the place was still a shell. Some crazy rich folks wanted to install a fancy-schmancy urinal in their third floor bathroom and nothing would ever induce her to find out why.

"Elva, haul the last urinal up to the top floor." Yves rolled a joint. Wyatt had his feet up on the dash.

Yves held out a bumpy joint to Wyatt. "You want one?"

Wyatt hesitated.

"It's all right if I'm offering." Yves said.

"You're messed up, man." Wyatt took the joint and lit up. He looked at Elva. "You've got this, right?"

"Right." Elva eyed him. Wyatt was a serious threat to the human gene pool. There had to be some way to work a lame intergalactic villain into her fanfic that would come to a red shirt end for his bumbling crimes.

Elva found the remaining lone urinal braced up against the wall of the van with bungee straps. She unhooked them and slid the box across the floor. At the edge, she jumped out of the van and lifted up the box. She grunted at the weight. Wyatt and Yves were laughing up front. The smell of pot leaked out the cracked windows. Why couldn't they help her unload this dang thing? Anger stewed in her chest.

She tottered, navigating up the front steps and toward the front door. That's when she saw the Bronco parked on the far side of the house.

Mitch.

The sounds of saws, hammers, and drills buzzed throughout the house. Where was he? Did she even want to see him? He'd never called her when he said he would. He wasn't into her, so why did she even care?

But she did care.

Elva headed up the stairs, stopping under some scaffolding. She glanced upward and found him. Mitch was high on a ladder and had his shirt off.

He was sawing above his head. The long reciprocating blade cut into the wood like butter.

Elva marveled at his master skill. She couldn't saw over her head without extreme threat of injury to her life and limbs. She put down the urinal and watched the ripples in his shoulders. She noticed how sweat drizzled down his back. She was hyper-aware that his chest was hairier than she expected it would be. Yes, Mitch's chest hair deserved serious thought. It was worthy of a lingering look.

A great iceberg of meaning hid underneath her primal want, a hunger for deeper things thrummed inside her—a need to be more than friend, to feel safe, to be transparent, to wholly know someone. She longed for that merging of psyches, more than physical, and yet physical. A transcendent connection. Her heart thumped in her chest. What would Mitch do if he could hear her thoughts? She wished mind melds were more than fiction.

Elva sighed. Her arms ached. She had to get this urinal installed or she was never getting home. She lugged it upward toward the bathroom on the third floor. Mitch never looked down. He kept carefully cutting rectangular chinks out of the 4x4s overhead to make a route for the electrical wiring. Each chink fell with a thud. Two steps up the second flight, an incontrollable impulse came over her.

"Hey, Mitch," she said, not knowing that she would regret those words for eternity.

The whole flow of time blipped in that moment and started again in slow motion. Mitch looked down at her. Elva met his friendly, albeit startled gazed. The sawzall began to grind and then it shuddered and twitched at the same time.

It happened so fast.

The sawzall twisted out of Mitch's hands. A swath of blood splatted her face. She stared up in a split second of horror, but then she immediately dropped the urinal box. It tumbled downward, breaking open, the urinal shattering. She whipped out her cell phone and headed for him.

Mitch had cut off his nose.

24 SAVING THE NOSE

Elva punched in 9-1-1.

The next seconds continued to inch forward in slow motion. Mitch's sawzall fell. It impaled the plank floor at her feet. The air filled with smoke and an acrid, electrical smell as the sawzall's engine burned to a halt. She didn't have time to contemplate the fact she'd nearly suffered her own serious amputation. She had to focus on the spurting blood and ignore Mitch's bloodcurdling screams.

She felt cool, wholly focused. A fortuitous memory from health class kicked to the front of her thoughts, and she engaged the hyperdrive. Elva undid her overalls and whisked off her t-shirt. She rushed up the ladder and pressed the shirt against the gaping hole on Mitch's face. She led him down while answering the 911 operator's questions.

"He's missing his nose," she said. "I'm helping him off the ladder."

Mitch trembled, and Elva put her arm around his bare shoulders, guiding him to the floor. He stopped screaming and whimpered in pain.

"You'll be fine, Mitch." Her voice was even, strong, powerful. Her composure stunned her. She'd shifted into an unknown gear of unfathomable capableness, something she didn't even know was inside her.

"You said he was missing his nose?" the operator asked. "Do you see it anywhere?"

"Hey, guys! I need help!" Elva yelled up to roofers.

Mitch's eyes were wild and tears streamed down his cheeks.

Elva held the wadded t-shirt in place and rested her hand against his bare chest.

"Mitch, the ambulance is on its way. Breathe, slowly with me," she said calmly.

Blood was splattered everywhere. She hoped he wouldn't pass out.

A guy from the roofing crew joined them.

"Find his nose," Elva commanded in a tone no one would disobey.

"Damn, if that ain't a nose," the roofer guy said, finding the bloody mass.

"Get something clean to wrap it in," she said.

The roofer ran for a first aid kit and returned, scooping the nose into a sterile glove and putting it into a cup. Elva stayed on the line with the operator who told her that the ambulance would be with them in a couple of minutes.

Elva moved her hand from Mitch's chest to the side of his face, forcing him to meet her gaze. She made a quick glance at heaven for the miraculous calm that was keeping her going.

"It's going to be OK." Elva caressed his hair. "Don't worry. The ambulance will be here any second."

But it was forever, dang it. The longest minutes in history.

She didn't move until the hands of an EMT covered hers.

"We'll take it from here, little lady."

Elva let go of Mitch and let the EMT take over. She sank on the landing and put her head between her knees.

"You need to move out the way, Miss," one of EMTs said.

She staggered downward.

"Will someone get her a shirt?" a fireman said from the bottom of the stairs.

Her considerable charms were exposed to the whole world. She crossed her arms across her chest to hide her boobs spilling out of her saggy bra. The bib of her overalls flapped around her knees. Her arms were crusted with Mitch's blood. She folded to floor in the black marble foyer when she reached the bottom. Shattered ceramic from the crushed urinal was scattered across the floor. Another fireman knelt beside her.

"Are you OK?"

"Somebody needs to get Mitch's nose," Elva said.

"It'll be taken care of." The fireman squeezed her hand. "You did a good thing here, saving that boy." He smiled at her reassuringly and then headed up the stairs. A minute later he helped the EMTs bring Mitch down on a stretcher.

Elva scrambled out of the way and watched them as they loaded the stretcher into the ambulance. Was Mitch going to be OK? Could they fix his face? They had to. A feeling of anxiety tightened around her chest making it hard for her to breathe.

Wyatt and Yves came into the house. Their eyes were bloodshot and wild. Elva crouched in the corner of the black marble entryway. She couldn't stop the shivering tremors.

She looked up. Wyatt was checking out her boobs. Special. If she could have punched him out, she would have.

"What happened to you, gal?" Yves tugged off his shirt and gave it to her. She took it gratefully and struggled to put it on. It was skin tight but comforting. The warmth of it helped her tremors to slow and then end.

"I hope Mitch is all right." Elva said.

"Who's that?" Wyatt asked.

"The guy on the stretcher," she said. "He cut off his nose."

"What the hell?" Yves's eyebrows rose.

She couldn't have said it any better.

"I guess the urinal will be coming out of my pay." Elva absently tucked loose strands from her ponytail behind her ears.

"I expect insurance will cover it," Yves said.

"Elva, are you cleaning this mess up?" Wyatt pointed at the ceramic pieces strewn across the floor. His words were slow and slurred. His words sent her temper near hot as a warp core breach.

"Hell, no," she spat.

"Cool down, Hicks. We're done here," Yves said. "Let's go pick up our paychecks and leave this crap for the insurance adjuster."

The ambulance was pulling away as they climbed into the truck. Yves pulled onto the street, and Elva picked at the crusts of blood on her arms and prayed Mitch was OK.

25 HOSPITAL

At home, Elva's phone didn't stop moaning out the *Star Trek* theme, but she didn't answer the calls. Papaw took them—some from the insurance company and some from work. She climbed into bed and curled on her side. Her stomach ached with worry about Mitch. This was her fault. She had just wanted to say hi. That's all.

She didn't look up when Papaw came to talk to her. Her phone was moaning again.

"Elva, are you going to take any of these calls? Your dang phone is giving me a brain tumor." Papaw held it out to her. The applied rhinestones caught the light and reflected rainbows on her wall.

Elva didn't move.

"Yves told Mr. Bob how calm you were when that boy sliced off his nose." Papaw said. "Hell, I think I'd have lost my lunch. Folks want to talk to you, gal. You're a real heroine."

The home phone rang in the living room.

"It's Mr. Bob." Nonny came to door. "He wants to talk to you, Pa."

Papaw went in the living room. Nonny sat on the edge of the bed and took Elva's hand.

"Nonny, can we go to the hospital and make sure Mitch is OK?" Elva asked.

"I'll see to it, honey."

Papaw came back with a grin on his face. "Mr. Bob says our insurance will cover the urinal as long as Mitch signs a release paper stating that Elva was in no way responsible for the accident."

"Pa, can we take Elva to see that boy," Nonny said, giving Elva a wink. "It might sweeten him up when it comes to the insurance papers."

"I guess we can do that," Papaw said.

Elva jumped out of bed and threw her arms around him. "Thank you. Thank you!"

"Let me get my flip-flops on," Nonny said. "I've got a tub of Red Vines and a six pack of Dr Pepper in the kitchen. We'll take them to him, poor boy."

"Good thinking," Papaw said. "If Elva don't soften him up, surely Red Vines and Dr Pepper will."

A few minutes later, Elva was on the bench seat of the pick-up between her grandparents. They took back roads into town instead of the highway. The ache of worry grew in Elva as they neared the hospital. Was Mitch's nose fixable? Would he ever

Plumb Crazy

forgive her?

Once inside, they spent a half-hour lost in a labyrinth of hospital hallways until they found Mitch's room. Elva was almost dizzy with fear, not knowing what to expect.

Papaw knocked on the door frame, but Nonny barged in. Elva followed.

"Elva Presley insisted on coming to see you," Nonny declared.

Mitch lounged in bed. Elva eyed him. His blobby swollen nose was reattached with a puckered jagged seam; it wasn't quite as bad as she thought it would be. Still it was pretty bad. What was she supposed to say to him?

Nonny placed the Red Vines and Dr Pepper on the bedside table. He clicked off the TV with the remote and smiled. His most delicious tummy was openly available for viewing, and Elva had to drag her eyes to his face.

Once she got past his nose, his eyes shocked her the most. In a good way. He was groggy, but his eyes were brighter than a galaxy. In them was a mix of wit and intelligence, giving her a weird feeling that this boy would listen to her, laugh at her jokes, and maybe, just maybe, understand her dreams.

She took a startled breath, and he noticed her noticing him, he noticed one hundred percent.

"We brought treats." Nonny popped the tab of one of the Dr Pepper cans and put it on the bedside tray. "I see they got your nose back on. It don't look

205

as dang awful as I thought it would."

Way to go, Nonny. Elva hoped a rogue space anomaly would suck her in immediately and deliver her from this embarrassment, but no such phenomenon was forthcoming. She didn't dare look into Mitch's eyes again. They unnerved her. Elva patted down her hair and tried to smooth her wrinkled shirt. Gosh, she sure needed to say something, but nothing came. She looked down, and her eyes landed on Mitch's almost perfect six-pack.

"Uh, uh, uh," Elva sputtered. "I'm sorry."

Mitch leaned forward, tilting his head. "I was hoping you'd come by." He patted the edge of his bed, motioning her to sit beside him.

Elva moved toward him like she'd been caught with a tractor beam. "Papaw, come with me down to the snack bar. They've got free milkshakes for senior citizens. I saw the sign when we came in." Nonny plumped up Mitch's pillow. "Let's give these two a chance to talk."

Papaw gave Mitch a long thoughtful look. "I suppose you're right. I do love chocolate milkshakes." He gave his belly a tap.

Nonny winked at Elva. Winked? Elva watched her grandparents leave.

She wasn't prepared for this. She liked the warmth she was feeling in Mitch's presence but was well aware this meeting was extremely complex. She intuitively knew their bonding could change them both, maybe forever. It was a tangible vibe. This kind of diplomatic situation was a job for someone trained, qualified, who understood basic societal rituals and how to apply them. A Star Fleet ambassador could handle this, not a plain old plumber gal.

"Thanks for saving my nose," Mitch said, breaking the ice for them.

The proper course of action seemed to be to respond.

"I'm so sorry about it getting cut off. I didn't mean to distract you. I swear it." Her voice vibrated with pain.

He blinked in surprise, and then his eyes softened. "Elva, this isn't your fault." He took her hand and stroked her palm with his thumb. "I shouldn't have been sawing over my head like a dang fool."

She looked away and bit her lip, still pained. His fingers moved to cup her cheek and guided her face back toward him. "It wasn't your fault." She turned her face into his calloused palm. It smelled of antiseptic and felt cool against her hot face. Another cosmic moment passed between them, drawing them together. She was transfixed by the green flecks mixed in with brown in his irises. They were that close.

"Does your nose hurt?" Elva didn't quite sit on his bed, but she leaned on it.

"I'm on a number of good pain killers," Mitch said. "I'll be here for a few days."

"Are your parents out of town?" she asked.

"No," he said. His hand slid from her face to his side. Elva waited for him to say more but he didn't. She forged ahead.

"I hope you aren't freaked out that I came by. My grandparents made me come."

No, that wasn't what she meant. That came out wrong. She could feel the tips of her ears heating up, and Mitch looked puzzled. If only she was a Betazed and could sense the emotions of the targeted alien, it might help this critical contact situation.

"I'm glad you came," Mitch said. "You saved my life."

And he smiled again. Yellow glints appeared with the green flecks in his eyes. She didn't know what they meant, not at all. Elva nervously poured a cup of water and gulped it down. She shifted from one foot to the other. Her eyes locked onto a pile of books by the bed.

"What are you reading?"

"Those are for school. My boss brought them from my apartment. I need to study."

"Are you in summer school?" she asked.

"I'm taking some Saturday classes at Lone Star College. I need to finish my homework."

"You're in college?"

"I'm in my second year," Mitch said.

"You don't look old enough to be in college." Elva picked at the blanket on his bed.

"I'm a senior. I'm enrolled in college and high school at the same time." Mitch smoothed down the blanket and his palm edged near hers and then came to a stop.

"Aren't your parents proud?"

"They don't even know. I'm emancipated."

"What the heck does that mean?" Elva reached to the bedside table and opened the tub of Red Vines. She pulled out one twisty red candy stick for herself and handed one to Mitch. Food was her drug of choice. Medicate. Medicate.

"Me and my parents split." Mitch took a sip of Dr Pepper and wrapped the Red Vine around his forefinger.

"Why?"

He swallowed. "My dad lives on the streets in downtown Houston. Mr. Bob calls him a retired plumber but he's really a drunk. Mom died of a drug overdose. I don't know the whole story. I lived in Boys City Children's Home for five years, and then I applied for emancipation when I was sixteen. I've been on my own ever since. I've had 'the disability of parents' removed. I'm independent. At least that's what the state of Texas says."

Mitch took a deep breath, like the effort of saying so many words was way overtaxing.

"Oh." Elva couldn't think of a thing to say. Nonny and Papaw had their quirks, but she didn't want to think about getting by on her own.

"I'm sorry," Elva said.

"Life is what you make of it," Mitch said. "I'm making plans."

209

"I've got a plan." Elva's words were too loud, too bright. This emancipation talk was revealing a piece of herself that she liked to keep under wraps, the "bock, bock, bock" chicken portion of her personality. She didn't know how to be emancipated, how to make it on her own. The odds were high that she would wind up in a dead-end job, wearing *National Enquirer*-sized pants and living in a broken down trailer. Nonny and Papaw were getting up there. She'd be alone. This wasn't something she'd ever admit to anyone out loud. Mitch was really brave. She wondered if she'd ever find that in herself.

Mitch reached out and turned over her hand. "I bet you've got an awesome future in front of you. Look at your fate line—how it lifts up from the base of your palm. It means you'll rise from obscurity to do something incredible."

There he went with his palm reading again. Elva pulled back.

"I don't know if I can believe that."

"What are you planning to do?" Mitch asked.

"I'm planning to write *Star Trek* novels for one." Again, Elva spoke with a shade of too much bluster. Her plan to write *Trek* novels seemed silly when she said it out loud. Her life plan felt as solid as the meeting of two tectonic plates.

"I remember that stack of papers you were scribbling on at the job out near Conroe. Were you working on a book?"

He didn't make one crack about her wanting to

be a writer. Gosh, basic acceptance was way better than fortune telling.

"It's a short story that I hope to expand to a novel someday," Elva said.

"You ought to bring it by for me," Mitch said. "I've got lots of time. I'll read it and let you know what I think."

"I'd like that," she said.

"Then it's settled."

"Mitch, I've got a question." She had to ask because his promises had been on the weak side up to now.

"What?"

"Why didn't you call me after the Fourth when you said you would?"

"I lost my phone with your number in it. Stupidest thing ever." He picked up a pen and a paperback copy of *Moby Dick*. He handed them to her "Write down the number for me."

Elva's hand shook as she scribbled her phone number on the inside cover. "Don't lose it this time."

"No way." Crinkles formed at the corners of his eyes as he smiled. She noticed that his hand shook when he took the book from her. Were his pain meds wearing off? A knock at the door interrupted them. A nurse dressed in pink scrubs came in. When she saw Elva, she smiled.

"I thought you said you didn't know any girls," the nurse said. She carried a small plastic cup on a tray and inside was a black blobby thing.

"Elva saved my life." Mitch's voice was so warm. She knew from the heat in her cheeks that her face was Rome apple red.

"It was nothing," she said.

"You're wrong about that." Mitch smiled and took her hand, his fingers sliding between hers. Her heart did a flump instead of a regular beat. Right at that moment the nurse placed the black blobby thing on Mitch's nose.

"What's that?" Elva asked.

"A leech," the nurse said. "Its blood-sucking action helps restore normal circulation."

Elva untangled their fingers.

"I'm tired." Mitch's shifting eyes betrayed his embarrassment.

Elva stared at his nicely clipped toenails, avoiding the blood-sucking leech at all costs.

"I'm going computer shopping at the mall. I have to go." Elva skittered out of the room like a frightened crawdad. She didn't even give him a chance to say goodbye. He'd have to understand— the leech and all.

Elva made her way to the cafeteria where she found Nonny and Papaw finishing chocolate shakes. Nonny gave Elva a piercing stare but didn't ask about what she and Mitch were talking about for so long.

"Papaw, can we go by the mall, the big one on the highway?" Elva asked, crossing both her fingers. She'd have crossed her toes but she was wearing flip-flops. It was WAY past time she got a laptop and moved forward with her *Star Trek* dreams.

"We have time, and I've wanted to try out that new fangled sweets bar," Nonny said. "I've heard they have double sour cherries and watermelon flavored cotton candy. I want to try both."

"We can do that," Papaw said.

"Let's go," Elva said.

The best plumbing upgrade she'd seen up to this point was in reach. She was finally, finally, buying an Apple MacBook. Holy snappin'!

26 SHANGRI-LA

Elva entered Apple Shangri-La at the mall just a half hour before closing. The sleek cases of the laptops were surrounded by dozens of the worshipful. The MacBook of her dreams was priced slightly over a thousand, had stereo speakers, and a backlit keyboard. Thorough satisfaction rushed down to her toes when she handed over her wad of wilted bills. She nearly squealed in happiness as the sales clerk handed her the white bag with the forbidden fruit silver apple with a half moon bite out of it. She was the proud owner of a new laptop.

She carried the Mac like a treasure through the mall and joined her grandparents, sitting at one of the café tables in the back of the candy bar. The aisles were lined with a rainbow of confections:

gobstobbers, jelly beans, chocolates, and hundreds more, but Elva wasn't even temped, not even by the *Star Trek* original cast Pez collection. The exposure to Apple radiation had greatly weakened her attraction to sweets.

"Did you finish your shopping?" Nonny held out a huge puff of cotton candy. "They've got every flavor here. This is strawberry."

"I'm done." Elva took the pinch of the spun sugar. It clung to her teeth like concrete.

She was too tired to set up her computer when they reached home. She placed it beside her bed and then rolled under the covers. She fell right asleep but woke a few hours later with her feelings tangled like angel hair spaghetti.

Whatever was going on between her and Mitch seemed meaningful but messy, different than what she'd imagined meeting a special someone would be like. She wanted so much—a friend, a soul mate, a lover.

Yep, she was hoping for the moon, sun, stars, the whole dang universe, and here was Mitch instead.

She shivered. The nose amputation haunted her. He shouldn't have sawed over his head, but she should have never said anything either. The blobby leech on the tip of his nose had been worse than any horror flick. And yet the possibility of Mitch flooded her, leaving her deliciously happy and carsick at the same time. Was he the nebulous man of her dreams? Maybe. Maybe not.

Heck, how do you know a thing like that? But she was sure of this: he liked her. In the scheme of things this was one humongous step for her social life, one stratospheric leap for Loser Girl kind. That thought chased her back into sleep.

The next day, Elva slept in. Mr. Bob gave her off the whole weekend. She'd pulled out the MacBook and was about to power it up when Nonny called her into the kitchen. Nonny'd placed a perm kit, a sack of colored rods, and a box of wrapping papers on the table.

"I haven't done my hair in months, Elva. Help me roll it."

"Sure, Nonny." Elva's Mac would have to wait. She hadn't rolled one perm since Nonny's layoff from the elementary school. Elva took a rat-tailed comb and parted out a thin strip of Nonny's limp salt and pepper hair.

"You're such a heroine, Elva Presley. I knew the day you were born you were destined for greatness. I sure named you right."

"I just tried to help." Elva carefully folded an end paper over the section and rolled it onto a tiny plastic rod.

"That's what you're always doing." Nonny handed Elva another roller. "I'm sorry about the goats falling on your shoulders these last weeks."

"Don't worry about it." Elva wrapped another section of hair and began to roll.

"It ain't. When poor Mimi died, I couldn't help thinking of your mama's wild spirit. Willa Jo was determined to bring you into the world against all reason. It hurt me bad when she went to the angels, but God bless her, she left one with me." Nonny patted Elva's leg.

"Uh, huh." Elva bit down on the comb and rolled another section. She didn't let Nonny see her tears and carefully wiped them away on her sleeve. Nonny was dealing with her baggage, a rare occurrence even with Zoloft. In this moment, Nonny was exactly who she should be, and Elva held to it as tight as she could.

In life, there were no guarantees, none. She grabbed for every log, broken chair, and chicken coop floating by in this flood called life. Fanfic was one of the things she was hanging onto, a life preserver. Plumbing cash lifted Elva up, getting her off the ocean floor of nothing, and up into the cerulean sky. It really helped that Nonny was along for the ride.

Elva kept rolling Nonny's hair. Her grandmother grew sleepy, and her head began to loll around like a bobble-head doll.

Suddenly Elva's phone sounded and she tried to muffle the *Star Trek* theme in a towel, but Nonny jerked awake anyway.

"I ain't got time to sleep." Nonny coughed. "I want to look nice for the award ceremony tomorrow. The mayor of Belling called, did I mention it? Mayor Bowdre is giving you a letter of commendation for helping that boy."

What the heck? Elva took a steadying breath.

217

"When is this happening?"

"They plan to honor you at a reception at the library tomorrow afternoon," Nonny said.

"You're not working," Papaw said, joining them. "You'll get your award, and then I'm taking you to dinner."

She was receiving an award for heroism—crazy, amazing, with a side helping of terrifying.

"I'm so proud of you." Nonny leaned over the sink and squirted the permanent solution into her hair. Elva coughed and wiped her eyes. The home perm solution made the house reek like a toxic waste dump, but in a good way.

She checked her phone. It was Mitch who had called! Her fingers hovered. Should she redial? Wait? She closed the phone and put it back in her pocket. She needed more time to process and no was way she telling him about the award. She texted Margarett and Shay instead. Margarett was at a church meeting and couldn't talk, and Shay hadn't answered since the Sonic episode.

Finally she snuck into her room to turn on her Mac. It worked like this: plug and then yay! The new Mac doused her in good karma. It was tangible evidence of her arriving life and helped balance out the nose amputation nightmare. Mac energy infused her with di-lithium crystal power.

Elva transferred the working fanfic file to her Mac. It was time. She readied to post her story on her blog and link it to her favorite fanfic sites. The current story just needed a few tweaks. She'd be done in no time.

She abandoned her desk and curled up in her bed, propping the Mac on a pillow. Her fingers pounded the new keyboard. None of the keys crunched or stuck as she tapped them. She'd never worked so fast in her life. She dove into a difficult section of her story. The last bit needed before she could post. T'Pak had just won a production award from the water reclamation bosses.

"Father, I don't wish to attend the award ceremony," *T'Pak protested strongly.*

"It is logical," Captain Spock said. "You must perform your duty."

"It's not logical," T'Pak's grandmother, Amanda, tilted her regal head. "You feel this is being forced on you. You are part human. You need to listen to that part."

"Neither of you understand." T'Pak groaned, placing her hand on her forehead. "I'm human, Vulcan, and Betazed. How am I supposed to balance such tangled DNA?"

In the end, T'Pak's arguments were ignored, and Captain Spock and her grandmother forced her to attend the award ceremony, an almost religious event.

Elva grunted. The story still didn't feel authentic. She snapped shut the Mac in absolute aggravation. A stream of breath flowed in and out of her mouth as she practiced her deep breathing to calm herself. The story wasn't polished enough. It would have to wait another day.

She turned off the light and snuggled under the covers. She was nodding off when her phone buzzed. She turned on the light and looked at the number.

Mitch.

It was three in the morning.

"Hello?" Elva answered, shaking away sleep.

"Elva, I woke you, didn't I?"

"I just started going down." A surge of adrenaline hit Elva, waking her totally.

"Sorry for calling so late. I won't keep you. Did you buy your computer?" he asked with a sheepish tone.

Had he trumped up a reason to call her?

"I did," Elva said. "A Mac. It's better than I ever expected. I've worked on my story like crazy tonight, but I didn't quite finish it." Her words came fast like fluttering moth wings.

"Good. Bring a copy so I can read it."

"I will." Elva said.

An awkward pause followed.

"It's good to hear your voice," Mitch said.

"You too."

"I'll see you soon, dove."

Dove, he called her dove.

Click.

Like she was ever going to sleep now.

27 AWARD

She slept in until noon. Elva barely had time to get dressed before her grandparents hauled her to the library ceremony.

"Hi, Elva." Mrs. Cook, the librarian, greeted her in the meeting room. "Are you excited about your award?"

"I guess," Elva said. "I'm not sure I deserve it. I did what anybody would do."

"Don't be so modest, dear," Mrs. Cook said. "I'm not surprised that you're being awarded for quick thinking."

"Really?" Elva plucked a strawberry from a plate next to a punch bowl.

Mrs. Cook smiled. "You're destined for great things."

"Why, thank you." Elva preened under the

praise. In her whole life no one had ever cast her in the same role as her mother Willa Jo. It shocked her and made her smile at the same time. The award ceremony went off without a hitch.

Two other people were also honored for deeds done for the community. Mr. Belling received an acrylic brick for philanthropic efforts. He'd paid for garbage cans to grace Belling's only park, and there was a similar award for Mrs. Davis who had scattered wildflower seed beside the train trestle. Elva's actions, though heroic, didn't warrant an acrylic brick.

Nonny cried appropriately when the mayor of Belling called out, "Elva Presley Hicks, Honored Citizen." The mayor handed her a rolled-up sheet of paper tied with some leftover Christmas ribbon. Elva thanked him, Mrs. Davis, her parents, Mrs. Cook, and the five families with two dozen kids between them that had come for the cake. Nonny couldn't stop clapping. The fact that Elva had been tacked on as an afterthought meant nothing to Nonny, and Elva loved her for it.

After the awards, they drove to Don's Truck Stop.

"Would you like a slab of chicken-fried steak and their good gravy to celebrate?" Papaw took off his baseball cap and smoothed back his iron gray hair.

She paused and said tentatively, "Sure."

Papaw got out of the truck and headed around to help Nonny. Elva followed her grandparents into Don's. Elva's eyes watered from the strong smell of the grill and slowly adjusted to the murky light.

"Hi, Elva." Shay came out of the kitchen. "How're y'all doing?" She led them to a booth.

"I'm good." Elva sat and the faux leather seat squeaked. She hadn't seen Shay since the ill-fated Sonic conversation.

"Anything going on?" Shay pulled a pencil from behind her ear. Her words were clipped and all business.

"I've been working hard on our *Star Trek* story." Elva smiled. "I bought a MacBook and the Internet is next. Then I'll post our fanfic." She flipped open the menu.

"That's interesting," Shay said, her voice dripping with boredom. "And what will you have to drink this afternoon?"

"Sweet tea," Papaw said.

"And a Shirley Temple for Elva Presley." Nonny saw a ginger ale with a splash of grenadine syrup and a maraschino cherry as the height of elegant sophistication.

"Did you hear me?" Elva asked. "I've bought a MacBook, and I'm posting our story."

"I heard you." Her voice dripped with boredom.

Elva gave Shay a lifted eyebrow, a real Spock look.

"I'll be back for your order when I bring your drinks." A rowdy bunch of Little League players entered the restaurant, and Shay hurried away.

Elva watched her go. Make-up caked over Shay's cheeks. Her nails didn't look chomped. They were long, fake, and painted deep red, so not Shay. They needed to talk. Things had changed and information needed to be put on the table. That's what friends did. Elva opened the menu again. Food always calmed her. She poured over the hot Buffalo wings, onion rings with bleu cheese, catfish with hushpuppies, and the beckoning chicken-fried steak.

Shay returned, juggling three mason jars. She plunked them on the table.

"Do you know what you want?" Shay asked.

Papaw ordered a T-bone, and Nonny asked for the catfish platter.

"Elva's having the chicken-fried steak," Papaw said.

Elva looked over the curled edges of the menu and grinned.

"You know that's got a gazillion calories." Shay tapped her pencil against her pad.

Elva looked up at Shay in surprise. In all their years of friendship, Shay'd never said anything about Elva's food.

"Since when do you care about what I eat?" Elva asked.

Challenging food choices of the Loser Girls of the Universe was breaking one of the fundamental universal laws that bound the sisterhood.

"She's a growing girl," Nonny said.

"Have you looked at her recently?" Shay asked.

"She's lost weight. This is the first time ever. Do you want to mess it up?"

It was like an alternate-universe-Shay, the one from the evil universe, the popular Shay who mocked fat girls had appeared; but this was no evil twin. There had been no transporter accident.

"Hey," Elva said. "Lay off my grandmother."

Nonny had the look of a wounded buffalo, but she didn't protest. Papaw stuck his nose in a *Thrifty Nickel* newspaper and wholly ignored their conversation.

"I'm trying to help you out. You don't want to be fat forever." Shay tapped her order pad again.

"Gosh, we've been best friends since the second grade." Elva twisted her napkin and stared at the salt shaker. "I can't believe you said that."

"Look, Elva, I can't talk like this at work. Forget about it. Let's talk about something else. Are you ready for Margarett's wedding?" Shay dropped the chicken-fried-steak-is-blubberizing-you talk, but she didn't say she was sorry.

"Whatever. Yeah, I'm ready." Elva couldn't mask her annoyance.

"Elva Presley will look so beautiful." Clueless Nonny put in. "Her dress is peachy pink and poofy. It's like made for a fairy princess."

"Mine's the same color," Shay said.

"Oh, I can't wait to see you two." Nonny reached across the table and pinched Elva's cheek.

"Could I have some more sweet tea?" Papaw had chugged the whole quart.

"I'll have it right up," Shay said. "Let's talk later."

Shay walked away. Good riddance. The space-time continuum was ripped! Shay'd have to apologize before this whole thing was set right.

Elva's grandparents sipped their sweet tea, and Elva slid out of her seat, making a path to the jukebox. Food wasn't coming fast enough. Country twang might even her out. She selected her favorite singles and added Elvis's "Jailhouse Rock" for Nonny. When she got back to the table, Shay was placing the huge white platters of food at each place. The chicken-fried steak was bigger than the plate.

Elva didn't say a word to Shay.

"Did you know that Elva Presley is a bona fide heroine?" Nonny asked.

"No, I didn't." Shay refilled their mason jars.

Elva crossed her arms. She'd texted a message about the ceremony.

"She saved a boy who cut off his nose at work. His name was Mitch," Nonny said. "I'm so proud of her."

"That's a story I'd like to hear, Elva." Shay gave the table of yelling Little Leaguers a desperate look but smoothed her apron and put on her cheery, how-may-I-help-you smile and headed over.

Elva stabbed the crunchy steak with her fork. Thick white gravy flecked with real peppercorns drizzled off the massive mound of mashed potatoes. She cut the steak in half and pushed it over.

"Do you want that?" Nonny asked.

"No," Elva said and lifted the half-steak and placed it next to Nonny's pile of catfish nuggets.

"Pass the pepper, gal," Papaw said.

Elva slid over the pepper and focused on her chicken fried steak.

28 THE SCORE

The next week of installing fixtures zoomed by. She managed to squeeze in a precious hour for shopping on Wednesday, yielding a printer, and a router, but she didn't have time to figure them out. Elva also didn't get back to the hospital. She and Mitch kept in touch with text updates and on Friday this came through:

I'm home from the hospital.

Her fingers hovered over her phone's tiny keyboard. Should she boldly go?

Yes.

Send me your address. I'll drop my story by.

She GPSed his address. His apartment was in Katy by the outlet mall. All she had to do was convince Papaw to drive her, and then find the time to drop by. On Friday, she was still on urinal duty and installed each ceramic fixture with methodical precision. She could put in an entire restroom with a full set of sixteen classic ceramic Kohler urinals in a day. Elva liked to work fast, to keep busy. It made her feel powerful. She wiped sweat from her forehead and stretched. Scorching heat was radiating through the thin walls of the building.

At lunch, her phone popped up a text.

Why haven't you come by? Mitch.

Sry. Been busy. Tomorrow for sure. Elva texted. By gosh, she meant it. She crossed her heart and hoped to die. She spent the rest of her lunch writing a few pages longhand, some last notes to perfect her story.

They finished at the jobsite early. Yves was eager to get home to watch a big Fight Club bout. Wyatt rolled up the electrical cords, and Elva flattened the urinal boxes, and they headed to the shop.

Papaw was waiting.

"You're gal is a fast trimmer." Yves complemented her as she climbed into Papaw's truck.

"I told you she'd work out." Papaw nearly crowed.

A feel-good rush spread through her. Did Papaw have any clue what he'd done for her by getting her this job? Did he know how much it meant to her that he was so proud?

"I picked up your pay from Mr. Bob." Papaw

handed her the rubber-banded bills. Her spirit was bolstered with the ultimate satisfaction of over two thousand dollars in one chunk. They'd worked crazy hours over the past week.

That night she tried to hook up the printer again, but it didn't work. Without it, she couldn't print out the manuscript for Mitch. Dang it.

The next day she caught the break she'd been hoping for.

"Mr. Bob called," Papaw said. "We're staying home. Somebody vandalized the truck tires at the shop. He's giving everyone the weekend off."

She'd go to the library, print off her story and then drop it by Mitch's. Perfect.

She texted him. *Are you home? I can drop my story by today.* How exactly she'd do that was still a complete mystery to her, but she was going to do it.

Seconds later her phone bleeped. *Sure.*

Elva begged Nonny to go with her to town, and for once Nonny relented. Elva scooched behind the wheel and shifted into drive. Driving made the world seem so open, like endless possibilities waited around every corner. She had to put "buying a car" on her to-do-list.

"I'll pick you up in an hour." She dropped off Nonny at Wal-Mart and gave her ten dollars for McDonalds while she headed to the library. She pulled into the parking lot and headed inside with her Mac. No more carrels for her. She checked her favorite fanfic ezines and bulletin board sites without slow crunching or the threat of an Internet time-out black screen of death. Elva surfed to her favorite GAFF sites, currently rich with the worst Classic *Trek* ever. Who in their right mind would mix the *Star Trek* and *Star Wars* universes? No way was Uhura ever hooking up with Luke Skywalker.

Elva looked around the library. She loved this place. Even though she'd upgraded her technology at home, she planned to keep coming here. The ambiance of the books and Mrs. Cook's encouragement were things she couldn't give up.

She printed out *The Death Incident.* Mrs. Cook didn't say a word when Elva printed 17 pages over the library's free print limit.

Mrs. Cook was a saint for sure.

Elva's plan of world domination of the *Star Trek* universe was firmly in place, and her splashy fanfic entry into fandom was to be better orchestrated than any shuttle launch. Plumbing cash had brought so much into Elva's reach. Mitch was going to be blown away by her story. Sure he'd have a few notes to improve *The Death Incident*, and she'd make the tweaks. Then snap, bam, her story was going out there.

She filled up the gas tank and then picked up Nonny at Wal-Mart.

"I need to drive into Katy to see Mitch. Please?"

"I don't want to drive out there." Nonny frowned.

"I bought the gas, and I'll do the driving, plus I'll stop at Buc-ee's for treats."

Nonny smiled. "Sounds good."

Elva pulled onto the highway and gunned the engine. Nonny settled in for a nap.

Elva's thoughts wandered on the open road. Papaw wouldn't understand this trip, but no matter, she loved him and in his way he loved her.

Near Mitch's apartment, Elva stopped at Buc-ee's and bought Nonny an extra-large Coke and crunchy corn Beaver Nuggets. Then she drove to Mitch's apartment complex. Nonny fanned her face and rolled down the window. Elva parked and let a 'I'll be right back" fly.

"I sweat like a hog in this heat," Nonny warned. "Don't leave me here too long."

Elva hurried to the complex gate, hugging her backpack with the precious copy of *The Death Incident* tucked inside. She could almost taste the anticipation of Mitch's reaction to her writing. She had no doubts he'd be amazed.

She texted Mitch. *I'm here.*

He texted. *On way.*

"Hi, Elva." Mitch opened the gate. He wore green shorts and a t-shirt.

"Your nose looks way better," Elva said. The swollenness around his nose had significantly decreased from their last meeting.

"It's reattached," Mitch said. "The leeches really helped." He led her along a winding path to his apartment.

"That's good." Elva wished the leech image could be permanently erased from her mind hard-drive. She followed him through a courtyard to his apartment door. Inside were a couple of chairs and a small TV in the living area. A folding table and chairs filled the dining area next to a tiny kitchen. She dropped her backpack on the table.

Mitch opened his fridge. "Do you want some juice or water?"

"I'm good. I brought my story. I've only got a few minutes to talk." She held out the sheath of papers. "Nonny is waiting in the truck."

"You could have emailed this." Mitch grinned and took the sheath.

"I like hand-written notes," Elva said. "And I'm having trouble with my router."

"I could come by and help." Mitch leaned back and smiled. "I can drive now."

"I'd like that." Elva pressed her hands against a mass of fluttery wings in her belly.

"Give me your address, and I'll come by tomorrow," Mitch said.

"All right." Elva nodded. Jittery excitement charged up her spine and ended up tingling in her ears. He handed her a pad, and she wrote down her address.

"I'll read your story tonight," Mitch said. "And give you my notes tomorrow, too. We'll set up your new system in no time."

"I have to go," she said. "Nonny can't take the heat."

"See you tomorrow," Mitch said.

Elva smiled and fumbled for the door. The shoelaces on her Converse tennis shoes had come undone, and she stumbled. Mitch laughed.

"You better tie those shoelaces."

Her heart did a double flump thing at that deep laugh. His aristocratic nose was a touch crooked now, but otherwise he was perfectly respectable date material. She closed the door and knelt down to tie the laces, and then ran like a bat-out-of-hell to the truck. Nonny had already started the engine.

Elva drove home, while Nonny dozed. All the while Elva solidified the next step on her life plan. She was going to really do it this time: post her *Trek* story. And woohoo! She had a date. Mitch had definite boyfriend potential. He was a *Seventeen* cutie even with a mutilated nose.

Her life was turning into a fairy tale, but there was no need for a fairy godmother. She'd completely put an end to the Cinderella crap. Elva earned her own money and needed no princely kingdom as a prop.

The only dark cloud hovering was over the goats. Papaw had called The Belling Meat Market and they told him they'd butcher the goats on the first week of August. The next day Elva called them back and told them that it was a mistake—no goats were coming their way. How would she tell Papaw she'd never send Bones, Christine, and M'Benga to the meat market?

The impossible was her thing, but this seemed beyond even amazingness. What words would change Papaw's mind? She had to figure them out. But how?

That evening, Elva got the printer working and began moving files from her desktop over to her Mac and her phone rang. It was Shay. They hadn't talked since the day Elva got her heroism award.

"Hi, Elva."

"Hi." Elva's jaw tensed.

"How've things been going?" Shay's voice was kind.

"Fine."

"Stop the nonsense," Shay said. "We need to talk. Bobby Ray is bringing me to the Volunteer Fire Department Barbeque tomorrow. Let's hang out. Margarett and Chase are coming too. It'll be like old times. Bring the fanfic and we'll work through a few pages.

"I've got something to do tomorrow," Elva said. "A friend is coming over."

"Bring her," Shay said.

"It's a guy."

"Oh, then bring him. Why not?" Shay asked.

Elva didn't answer at first. Why not? Because The Loser Girls had disbanded, though no one was willing to say so. She'd done everything she could to lead them toward better things, but things had changed forever. Now she wasn't sure she wanted to be friends with Shay or Margarett. Shay was turning into a hard-edged person that Elva didn't understand at all, and Margarett was getting married. And worse, they both treated her like she was the one who was lagging behind and not getting anything, like her efforts were nothing.

"Elva, are you there? We stick together no matter what," Shay said. "It's our way."

Elva had to honor that. There was no choice really. They had survived high school hell and had written fanfic. That meant something. She wouldn't toss their friendship out because things were changing. She'd give it a chance.

"OK, I'll come," Elva said.

"What's your friend's name?" Shay sounded curious and open, not like the last time they talked.

"Mitch."

"Isn't that the guy you saved?"

"Yeah."

"It'll be great to meet him." Someone spoke to Shay in the background. "Hey, my break is over, Elva, but thanks for not hanging up on me first thing. I sort of deserved it."

"No problem." Elva sighed, finally an apology.

"I'll see you later."

As soon as the call ended, Elva's phone rang again.

"So, you're coming!" It was Margarett this time. "Shay just texted me."

Shay texted faster than light speed.

"I'm coming," Elva said.

"You have a date?" Margarett asked.

"Sort of."

"That's fantastic," Margarett said. "There's a carnival and you can win cakes. The three of us back together again. It's been too long."

"It has been a while," Elva said.

"I can't wait for tomorrow!" Margarett clicked off and Elva stared at the phone. Margarett's voice was so jubilant. Absolute stupidity seemed to be working for her.

Elva's phone buzzed yet again, buzzed with incoming texts. What did Shay want?

But it wasn't Shay, Mitch texted her.

U there? Red ur stry.

Did u lik it? He'd read it at light speed.

Calling u now.

The notes of the classic *Star Trek* theme followed.

"Hi, Elva," Mitch said.

"Hey, Mitch." Elva leaned back on her bed. She was talking to a boy in bed! Now this was boldly going where she had never gone before.

"I finished your story," Mitch said.

"Didn't you just love it?" she asked. "I love the part where Spock has to accept the fact that his daughter is dating a Gorn. Isn't it awesome?"

"Yeah," Mitch's voice wavered.

"Mitch, what's wrong?" Elva asked. "You sound funny."

"I'm good. My meds are still making me fuzzy-headed at times."

"Oh," she said. "Did you have anything else to say about my story?"

"It was … interesting," Mitch said. "I can honestly say that I've never read anything quite like it. And, um, uh, the setting, the setting was very good."

"The setting? That's not what's important!" Elva

kicked her leg against the bed. "Didn't you just love the inter-species romance?"

"Yeah, it was, um, you know … " Mitch's voice sounded funny again, quivering-like.

"It sounds like you didn't like it." Elva couldn't hide the hurt or surprise in her voice.

"No, that's not it. It takes me time to put my thoughts together. There was some good stuff."

"Are you sure?" Elva could feel a rogue knife of major loser girl twisting in her belly.

"You want me to be honest, don't you?" His voice pitched lower.

"Of course I want you to be honest." She pressed against the sharp pain poking at her insides. Elva was genuinely baffled by his lukewarm reaction. She had put the truest most powerful emotions she could think of on those pages. What could possibly be wrong with her story?

"I'll bring my notes when I come over tomorrow," Mitch said. "You can read them and tell me what you think."

"Um, great. I got the printer working and I'm setting up the router now. Still you could go over the system and make sure I did it right."

"I'll be there, Elva." She loved how her name sounded when he said it.

"I plan to hang out with my friends tomorrow too," Elva said. "Do you want to go with me?"

"Sure. Sounds fun. I haven't made any plans, and I'm caught up with my economics homework."

"I'll see you in the morning."

"It's a date," Mitch replied.

Elva hung up the phone and gave herself a hug, letting her mind move into an out of body experience. A wave of nirvana flooded her with a clear vision of the pearly gates of heaven at the same time.

OMG.

It was a date, a real date. Mitch had said, "It's a date."

The score? Universe = ∞. Elva Presley = 1.

29 CRITIC

Sunday arrived with no fanfare.

Papaw left early with Nonny for a swap meet in Houston and wouldn't be home till late. Elva lurked on the edge of forever waiting for when Mitch would knock. Terror roamed around like a bobcat in her belly. What if she was misreading the waters again? What if he saw her hick shack in the country and high-tailed it and ran? And the most terrifying thought—what if he stayed? What would she do with that?

Bottom line, today, she would be alone with a boy in her own home for the first time.

Sunlight slanted through the living room window as Elva stretched into warrior's pose. Her arms rose to the sky. Her front leg bent, and her back leg was straight. She balanced and turned her face into the light.

Elva arched her back and whispered to the sun, "Help me make this work out?"

She stepped out of the pose. Enough yoga, she thought, reaching for her nail kit under the couch. She selected her fire engine red nail polish and was on the pinky toe when Mitch pulled up in his Bronco.

"I'm in the house," Elva hollered through the screen door. It was an unseasonably cool morning.

"What are you doing?" Mitch stepped up the concrete steps, opening the door.

"Painting my toenails," she said.

Something flitted in Mitch's eyes. Unfathomable. What did it mean? The look flitted away so fast that she didn't have a chance it figure out, but she was sure it was a good sign, absolutely sure.

Mitch carried a large manila envelope. He let the screen door snap shut.

"I've brought your story," he said. "The notes are on it if you care to take a look." He nervously rocked on the heel of one scuffed Roper and then on the other, leaning against the wall. His thumbs hooked his belt loops.

"I'll read them later," she said. He had to have liked most of it. Mad desire to savor his words of praise swarmed in her, but she didn't want to seem too needy.

"Good plan."

"I have to feed the kids before we can leave," Elva said. "I promised Margarett and her fiancé

Chase we'd meet them at noon. My friend Shay will meet us after that. Does that work for you?" Elva's words tripped and flopped like bait fish, but Mitch didn't seem to mind. He moved beside her and sat on the coffee table, and then he smiled.

"Sure."

She smiled back. Her nerves came down ten notches, and she finished painting her toenails.

"So where are these kids that we have to feed," Mitch asked. "I didn't think you had brothers and sisters."

"I have goat brethren," she said, blowing on her toenails one last time. She hobbled into the kitchen on the heels of her feet. "The kids take two feedings every day. Nonny went into town with Papaw, so it's up to me. It's usually up to me."

"Let me know what I can do to help," Mitch said.

"Put my story next to the laptop in my bedroom," she said, pointing. "My room is through that door."

Elva peeked around the refrigerator to watch his cute butt disappearing into her room. Hallelujah, a real live boy in her bedroom!

"Whoa, sweet laptop," Mitch said.

"Plumbing is hell, but payday is Friday," Elva said. "I call my Mac a plumbing upgrade."

Mitch laughed as he rejoined her in the kitchen. "So how does one feed a goat?"

She bent over and touched the little piggy to make sure it was dry, and then she shuffled into her new flip-flops.

"Heat up the water, and I'll get the bottles ready."

Mitch nodded, and Elva got the nipples out of the dishwasher. He fumbled with the stove.

She rested a hand on a hip. "Only the back burners work."

A few minutes later Mitch and Elva were thigh to thigh on the breezeway steps. He fed Christine, and she had M'Benga and Bones on her lap, juggling their two bottles. She rubbed her face against M'Benga's bristly coat and covertly checked Mitch out. Except for the jagged red seam around his nose, his face looked excellent. He hugged Christine to his chest and smiled. A dimple appeared in his cheek, making her hyper-aware of an invisible thread pulled between them so tight that it was cutting into her heart.

"So what's the plan for the day?" Mitch asked.

"We're going into town to the Volunteer Fire Department's Barbeque at noon to meet my friends."

"Let me get your friends straight—Margarett and Chase are getting married," Mitch said, "And Shay works at the truck stop."

"That's right and Shay's dating, Bobby Ray. He's twenty-five and probably married already which is considerably ignorant too." Elva rubbed noses with M'Benga. "Love doesn't generally make sense."

"This is love?" Mitch looked at her cockeyed as he patted Christine's belly. He was a natural with goats.

"Well, maybe lust. When you're only sixteen or seventeen-years-old these things don't make much difference." Elva tried to sound wise but instead came across like a tribble. She set out alfalfa for the kids and filled their water trough. They were weaning the babies. Elva didn't want to consider what came next. She took the shovel and began scraping the concrete, shoving the balls of goat manure into a bucket by the door.

"Let me get that for you," he said.

A boy who would shovel manure for her, she shivered with the luck of it and took the pitchfork to spread the hay.

"We can head into town when we're finished here," Elva said. The goats gamboled through the breezeway and began to munch the sweet smelling stalks.

"Don't you want to set up your computer now?" Mitch asked.

"We'll do that after barbeque," Elva said. "I promised Margarett that we'd be there by noon."

"Then let's go," Mitch said.

"One sec. Let me brush my hair." Elva dashed inside and slathered on cherry lip gloss and checked her face in the mirror. Her complexion was perfect, no zits, nada. She lost so much weight there were faint hollows in her cheeks. Her eyes were good too. No dark circles. Her eyebrows! She plucked a few stray hairs.

Mitch called from the breezeway, "Are you coming?"

"On my way." As she headed out the door, she brushed against the manila envelope with her manuscript in it. She grabbed it and tucked it under her arm. There'd be time to peek at Mitch's notes on the way into town.

"You sure you want to bring that?" He pointed at the envelope. Christine butted her thigh, and Elva gently pushed the goat away.

"There might be time," she said.

Mitch shrugged. "OK, then."

They walked to his Bronco, and goose bumps, butterflies, and hot honey moved in the pit of her stomach when he idly twined his fingers with hers. He opened the door for her, and she climbed inside, trembling when his hand slid to the small of her back, guiding her onto the seat.

"Turn left, and then hang a right at the bridge." Elva said, as Mitch pulled onto the black-topped road. She folded her hands in her lap and crossed her ankles. They passed tall rows of corn and then a watermelon field. Striped green balls were scattered for acres.

"Watermelon looks good," Mitch said.

"Bumper crop," she answered.

That was the extent of their conversation into Belling. Even though they didn't talk, it was a comfortable silence, like words weren't that important. The "nose thing" had forged a potent bond between them. She was so alive, here and now. Astral connections (more Internet research) were afoot. Elva leaned forward and let the cold

AC blow on her face. She was hot, so hot.

"Turn left at the water tower." Elva pointed to the silver monstrosity at the edge of town. A blazing red painting of the Liberty bell and the script of Belling in blue proclaimed their high school team—the fighting Texas Rangers. Most of the stores in the old downtown were ghost shacks with sheets of plywood blocking the doors and windows. Nobody came to this part of town much since the bypass was built.

"All the money collected goes to supporting our local volunteer fire department."

"I figured that," Mitch said.

There was a line thirty cars long to get in the parking lot.

Mitch turned on the radio and kept time by tapping on the steering wheel. He turned off the air and rolled down the windows.

The wait was ten minutes at least. Elva casually opened the manila envelope with her manuscript and began to read Mitch's notes. She blazed through the first four pages, and as she read, her feelings for Mitch plunged from fire hot into an ice age. She'd expected a few suggestions, but this was WRONG!

Boring!

Unclear!

One-dimensional!

She would have beamed out of his truck right then and there if she could have.

Incomprehensible!

Check your grammar.
I'm not sure that anyone is interested in classic Trek anymore!

Mitch was humming with the resonating honky-tonk music. Elva flipped off the radio.

"You better turn this truck around and take me home," she demanded.

"What are you talking about?" Mitch asked.

"This." Elva managed to spit out through her clenched teeth. She slapped the manuscript on the dashboard.

"Hell, Elva, you asked for my opinion," Mitch said. "My honest opinion."

"Take me home." Her words were low and acidic.

"But," Mitch said.

"But, nothing." Elva cut back with a wedge of hysteria in her voice. "You get me home and now."

Ten minutes later they pulled up to her house. Mitch tried to turn on the radio a couple of times, but Elva kept flipping it back off. He tried to speak to her but she stared out the window and grunted in return. He'd broken her heart, right in two. Mitch was supposed to be the answer to her prayers. He was supposed to be the best thing that ever happened to her. She stared at him. His knuckles had turned white from gripping the steering wheel. The thread of connection between them had snapped. How could she have believed that anything good was coming to a Loser Girl? She opened the truck door as it crossed the bridge to her house.

"Keep the door shut until I stop," Mitch said.

Elva didn't answer but snatched up her manuscript and jumped out of the truck. She hit the ground running.

"Elva Presley Hicks, you're freaking me out! Chill!" Mitch called after her as she high-tailed it into her house. The Elvis painted on black velvet over the couch seemed to give her a mocking stare.

She threw herself down in her chair. Mitch had better ask his lucky stars to help him. She planned to break a mirror, walk under a ladder, cross a black cat's path, and dedicate the bad luck to him. She didn't have to read his daily horoscope to tell his fortune. "You will betray a close friend." How dare he write such biased, unfair criticism about her precious story? Oh, if he was the last guy on Earth it would be lights out for the human race.

Elva glared at the sea of red marks strung across her manuscript.

No way.

He was supposed to offer constructive criticism. This was a massacre.

"Study grammar!" She slammed the manuscript to the floor and leaned back in her chair, placing her palms on her eyes. He was so mean. She would never, ever, not under any circumstances go anywhere near someone who so clearly could not comprehend her artistic endeavors and was so shallow that he couldn't see the absolute relevance of classic *Star Trek.*

She'd thought Mitch was a kindred spirit. How could she have been so wrong?

Loser Girl karma was striking like a rattler. Darwin's theory of evolution was at work here. How dare she come against survival of the fittest? The universe was slugging back; the laws of survival determined that Loser Girls didn't get hotties. It wasn't possible for her to evolve beyond her manifest destiny.

She tried yoga breathing to calm her raging emotions.

Honestly, she should have heeded the red alert when Mitch had cut off his freaking nose right in front of her. That was a sign to back away if there ever was one! She touched her forehead. How could she be so stupid? Could she be suffering post-traumatic shock from when his nose had flown across the room in front of her? That single harrowing event must have harmed her psyche. She'd even contemplated him as a possible boyfriend!

Elva placed her right hand over her left and touched her thumbs in a cosmic mudra. When she got a job with actual health coverage, her first stop would be a mental health facility. She planned for her head to be shrunk and prodded until it was, well, absolutely "normal." Hopefully, her ample butt would follow the lead of her processed brain.

All afternoon, she continued to ruminate on the horror of it all, shoving her manuscript under the bed. Then she curled up on her mattress and pulled the sheet over her head. Would Mitch call her to apologize, and if he did, should she answer?

But he didn't call.

Margarett texted a couple of times, wondering why Elva hadn't shown for the barbeque. Nonny and Papaw called to say they were heading to an all-you-can-eat catfish buffet and would be home way late. Elva would have moped all night if not for a knock on the door around suppertime.

"Are you home?" It sounded like Shay but the voice was higher pitched and shaky.

"Shay, is that you?" Elva called.

"It's me," Shay replied. "I looked for you at the barbeque."

Elva rolled out of bed and meandered to the living room to unhook the screen door, scooping up two expired Hostess cupcakes off the kitchen table on the way. This was definitely a double cupcake day. She swung the door open, ready to dump her load of problems, but Shay's red-rimmed eyes had swathes of black mascara under them and stopped her short.

"Come on in, Shay," Elva said. "What's wrong? Are you're having trouble with Bobby Ray?"

Shay burst into tears. "Mama won't take me back. Bobby Ray's married, and I'm pregnant!"

"Have a cupcake." Elva held out one and bit back the "and you're surprised?"

"I don't want a cupcake," Shay wailed. "What am I going to do?"

"I'll get you some iced tea and saltines," Elva

said. "That'll help you feel better.

"I can't believe Bobby was just stringing me on." Shay moaned and sank back on the couch, and Elva went in the kitchen. When she returned she offered Shay the tea and saltines, and handed her a roll of toilet paper too.

Elva patted Shay's back as deep sobs shook her like earthquake tremors.

"You were right about Bobby Ray. Totally right." Shay blew her nose into a wad of toilet paper. "He's a no good snake. I couldn't see it. I wanted somebody to love me. Is that so stupid?"

It wasn't in the Loser Girl protocol to say I-told-you-so.

"No, it's not stupid," Elva said. "The right guy will come along for you. And in the meantime we'll figure out about your baby, I don't know anything about babies, but I promise—I'll help you. I mean karma owes us big time. I expect absolutely great things to come our way. Honestly."

"Do you really think so?" Shay sniffed and blew her nose again. Bits of toilet paper stuck to the floor.

"I do."

"Can you look up a good voodoo curse on the Internet?" Shay asked. "I want to get Bobby Ray good."

"Let's allow his evilness to slide this time," Elva said. "He is your baby's daddy and all."

Shay hesitated and then nodded. "You're right, being mean can't be good for Junior. Let's look at baby clothes instead."

Elva got her laptop and began searching designer baby clothes.

After looking over a dozen websites, Elva took a break to find Neapolitan ice cream in the freezer, and they ate it along with watermelon. Shay fanned in front of the AC and then threw up. She catnapped and Elva looked up teen pregnancy websites. She printed up a bunch of articles for Shay. She even ordered a book on eBay that was recommended on every best-of-pregnancy book lists she could find—*What to Expect When You're Expecting*.

She practiced her warrior pose and waited for the phone to ring. Mitch didn't call. Not that she really wanted to talk to him, but she wanted the satisfaction of not answering the phone. Margarett did call, wanting to know what happened to Elva, why she hadn't shown at the barbeque. Elva gave Margarett the low down on Shay. Margarett came right over with Chase. They brought a pizza with them.

Shay woke and ate some too. In the end, they watched reruns of the *People's Court* online into the wee hours of the morning.

30 JACK HAMMER

For the next few days, Elva jumped at her phone every time it beeped, but she didn't hear a word from Mitch. She hated to admit it, but she wanted to call him. The good news was she didn't have time because of work.

At night, she couldn't get to sleep. Bad dreams plagued her where the sawzall did way worse than cut off Mitch's nose. She fought those dreams by having Shay buy her a dream catcher at Don's. Elva hung it above her bed and the dreams improved, but the deep ache in her heart didn't. It was an impossible kind of pain. Mitch had been no user like Wyatt. He cared for her for real.

Down in the bottom of her heart a tiny voice whispered, "Maybe he had a point or two about your fanfic."

She shoved that thought into the far darkest corner of her mind. It hurt too much to think that the one pure thing that had come her way this summer—Mitch—she'd tossed out like the trash. Why?

Because he'd told her his truth.

Elva thanked God for the plumbing. The intensive trim work helped her hide from feelings too deep and too real.

The temperature shot up and hovered over a hundred, and her work hours equaled that number, too. They ran into Mitch's outfit, Bowers Heating and Cooling, at several jobsites. At first her stomach ached from the possibility of running into him. After the first week, her stomach ended up aching from the possibility of never seeing him again.

At the end of every day, Elva was so tired and overheated that most nights she skipped supper. Finally urinal duty ended when Big R Construction made a huge mistake at the valve plant. Slabs of concrete reinforced with steel rebar had been poured before the plumbers had roughed the pipes—an area that should have had Teflon piping for industrial applications.

Mr. Bob rented three jackhammers, and Elva spent the rest of week busting out concrete. Yves and Wyatt were both on the job with her. At first, she wasn't sure if she could handle a Milwaukee Breaker Hammer, but soon she realized being taken off trim work alleviated that feeling in her stomach that Mitch might show up any second. His outfit didn't work at the plant.

Jackhammering was rough work, but it was safe, even though the jarring of the jackhammer made her insides ache as much as her heart did. Yves said it was the worst kind of work and could damage the kidneys. She didn't know about the damaging your kidneys part, but knew it was hard on the stomach. She'd thrown-up multiple times a day.

The worst part of the work was hammering through the steel rebar used to reinforce the concrete. One time sharp metal wire back-lashed and scratched her leg. It took twelve of the big band-aids to cover the cut.

On Friday, they still had a good stretch of concrete left and were on such a tight time schedule that they didn't leave early to get their pay. She kept plugging, chipping bits out of the vast concrete slab and didn't think about the clock. Papaw drove up to the site to pick her up.

"Gal, it's almost midnight," Papaw said.

"I want to finish busting out the last five feet," Elva said.

"Time to lock up and head home."

She didn't argue. She glanced back at the trail of chopped concrete. It looked like a *Star Trek* horta had chewed through the slab. Several concrete chunks were even shaped like the horta's silicon eggs. She turned off the jackhammer and moaned, rubbing her lower back. The pain. The pain.

"Let it go, gal." Papaw's voice was gruffer than

usual.

She pulled off her dusty gloves. Powdered concrete covered her. She tapped her hard hat, and then brushed off concrete chips that speckled her now worn steel-toed boots and Dickies. Corrosive dust burned her eyes. Her left wrist was swollen, and she'd an ugly cut on her right hand. The cut was deep enough for stitches, but she didn't want to pay the emergency room bill. She'd dabbed on a huge glob of antibiotic gel from the first-aid kit and attached several butterfly bandages to close the wound.

"Here's your wages." Papaw handed her a stack of cash when they reached the truck. "You got a small bonus added from the insurance claim." Out came her passbook and she wrote down the new amount. Her savings account would reach over thirteen thousand dollars. Elva could buy a car, a brand new Kia, if she wanted.

31 BUBBA WALLER HOMES

After the week of busting concrete, Yves, Wyatt, and Elva were put on yet another crew. Wyatt had pinched her butt one afternoon, but he wasn't even a blip on her sensors anymore.

She'd evolved.

And in more ways than one. She was ready to post her fanfic. Mitch had temporarily derailed her, but that was the past and her eyes were fixed on the future. The goats' fate was still up in the balance, but her hope hadn't wavered. They'd land on the side of life.

Today she was headed with Yves and Wyatt to Galveston to pipe a pre-fab house. It took two hours of driving to reach the jobsite. At least Mr. Bob was letting them record the driving hours on their timesheets. She served as the ultimate go-for on the site. She fetched ladders, electrical cords, and joints of PVC pipe. Yves kept her running for every small tool he needed.

Near noon, the air above the blacktop road shimmered with heat, and she could taste a bite of salt. The rhythmic whooshing of the Gulf waves thrummed underneath the sound of a quick inland breeze. She always felt a celestial bond with the Gulf. Her mother's ashes were scattered in the white-capped water. She gazed at the rows of foamy yellow waves rushing onto the ecru sand. It wasn't the most beautiful place in the world, but the flat expanse of grayish-brown water turned to midnight blue at the horizon. Willa Jo was part of that eternity.

No one was ever fully lost. The wide Gulf attested to it.

She sighed and plugged in the chop saw and began to cut lengths of PVC for Yves up topside. The house was set on pilings. Plastic dust floated around her like a cloud. Yves was a lazy bones, and Elva had to haul each cut length of pipe up the stairs to him. She was so busy and the chop saw was so loud that she didn't hear anything, no breezes, no waves, and not the engine of an arriving vehicle. She'd hooked her tape measure on her belt and was chopping away when a rumbling voice by her ear sent an electric shock down her spine.

"Hey, Elva. I finally caught up with you."

Mitch.

She froze with the chop saw spinning in mid-air. No red-alert alarm had sounded inside her, or she would have manned battle stations. A cool hand covered hers and helped her lower the spinning 8-inch blade.

"I think we've had enough of saw drama to last a lifetime." Mitch gently pulled her hands back. The high hum of the motor slowed to a stop, but the blade continued to revolve.

Elva kept her eyes on the sharp teeth of the saw. She couldn't look into Mitch's eyes or she'd be lost for sure.

"I've got the safety on," she said.

Mitch took her hands and helped her to her feet.

"Boss Man, I was wondering if you could spare Elva for an hour or so," Mitch called up the stairs. He tipped back his Catalina hat and rested his arm around her shoulders. She fit into him, her head tucking below his chin. Yves came from overhead and Wyatt followed. They gave Mitch an appraising look.

"I guess I can let her go for an hour, but then you better have her back, or she'll have hell to pay from her Old Man," Yves said. "From me too."

"That's fire you've got there." Wyatt pointed at Elva.

Elva pulled down the bill of her baseball cap, shading her blushing face.

"I think I can deal with a little fire," Mitch said. He turned her in a circle and dusted off the plastic bits that had been thrown off by the saw.

"When are you asking *me* to go?" she asked.

Mitch shouted out laughing. "Right now. Elva Presley Hicks, I'd like to take you to Shrimp 'N Stuff over on Avenue O." He gave a slight bow. "Come with me?"

Elva cocked her head to the side and stared. Mitch's slightly lopsided nose twitched.

Why not?

"All right," she said.

She propped her boots up on the dash of his Bronco and leaned back as he rolled the windows down, and the sultry coastal air cocooned them. The Gulf stretched to their right. Here, the water faded to green and then darkened to blue with sparkling motes in the distance. It felt like a sign. Mitch turned off the seawall at the Goodwill and headed toward the restaurant.

Soon they turned into the narrow parking lot of a non-descript building. A small sign swung in the breeze—Shrimp 'N Stuff.

"They've got good fried shrimp here," he said.

Elva grunted and followed him across a weathered patio. Inside, twenty aged chrome dinettes were shoved together. A long walk-up counter was against one wall with an old-fashioned menu board above. The dining area was half full.

"You know how to take a girl out," she said.

"Wait 'til you taste the shrimp and hushpuppies."

Elva trembled when his hand slid around her waist and rested on her hip.

"We'll have two orders of fried shrimp, sweet tea, fries, and hushpuppies," he said.

The server handed Mitch a buzzer.

"You could have asked me if that's what I wanted."

"I don't just read palms. I'm a mind reader." Deep dimples appeared in his cheeks and he led her to a table in the corner, never moving his hand from her hip until they sat down. He took the chair opposite.

"Are you warming up to me yet?" he asked.

"No way," Elva answered. "It'll take more than a basket of fried shrimp."

"You're still mad about that story. You wanted sugar-coating, and I gave you ice water truth. Let it go." He leaned back in his chair, half-smiling.

She pushed the silver topped salt shaker in a slow circle. "Why didn't you call me?"

"Would you have answered?"

"Hell no."

"There you go." Mitch tapped the table and a silence like an immeasurable void formed. Light years in distance separated them.

The buzzer vibrated on the table.

Elva checked out Mitch's flat butt as he passed. What a freaking Loser Girl nightmare. She'd been dreaming about dating since the dawn of time, and here she was with a fish on the hook, and all she could think was, hell, throw him back. Dang, crappie, and she wanted a striped bass.

Mitch placed the basket of shrimp in front of

her. Elva reached out, grabbed a red tail, and crunched down on the fried goodness. Mitch took another shrimp, dredged it in cocktail sauce and took a bite. Their fingers brushed when they reached for the next morsel of shrimp. A jolt shot through her core.

"I'm posting my story tonight." Elva dredged a shrimp through the chunky tarter sauce. The words bubbled up on their own accord, but she knew when she said them it was true. She'd put herself out there for the whole world to see. *The Death Incident* was going online.

"Hell, you're still caught up on that?" Mitch asked.

He tapped the table in frustration. Elva took a bite of coleslaw.

"I wouldn't post if I were you." He tapped the top of her hand.

"Well, you're not me."

At least she was getting an out-of-this world meal. Elva loved the shrimp and hushpuppies. She loved the sweet iced tea. The key lime pie tasted like heaven on earth, but she didn't say any of this to Mitch.

"I'm ready to get back to my job."

"If that's what you want," Mitch said, catching a bit of meringue at the corner of her lip with his thumb.

Elva didn't answer and headed out the door.

When they pulled up to the jobsite, she folded her hands and said with an icebox chill, "Thank you for the meal."

Mitch stared at her, and she stared right back. It was like his will and her will were firing all phasers. Then he leaned in, slipped a crooked finger under her chin and planted the most impossibly perfect sweet tea, key limey kiss on her slightly chapped lips.

"You think about that," he said.

He planted another quick kiss—better than chocolate and possibly a number of popular illegal drugs—and then pulled away.

"Think about that long and hard, Elva."

She had to heave in a breath but managed to get out of the truck and stumble away.

Oh, she'd be thinking for sure.

32 LOL AND CRY

That night Elva finally, finally, fiiiinallly, posted her fanfic story and added links to it at every *Star Trek* site in the known universe.

She slept late the next morning and didn't have a chance to check the responses. The whole plumbing day was almost unbearable. What would be the reaction out there?

When she got home from work, she rushed to her blog and gasped. *The Death Incident* had 527 posted messages. Her blog had almost one hundred thousand hits in one day. She was a PHENOM. Her insides quivered. This was beyond any dang thing she could have possibly imagined. She clicked the comments and began to read.

Startrek Maven says:

LOL. So bad that I nearly threw up.

ClassicSpock111 says:

Fascinating. NOT. The only thing wrong with this story was the characters, plot, and theme—Spock's long lost daughter from a water reclamation planet becomes the ruler of the Gorn Hegemony. Oh, the Vulcanity. The grammar was OK.

TheGodofTREK says:

The worst classic TREK fanfic ever written. Makes Enterprise's final episode seem like a masterpiece. More snooze factor than Star Trek: The Motion Picture.

LosetheshirtKIRK says:

"Beam me up, Scotty. There is no intelligent life here."

BorgDrone4vr says:

The Borg rejects this human. This kind of crap should never be added to us. If so, the entire Borg collective would implode. This human must not be assimilated!

That was enough. She checked Twitter and, yes, the tweeting was out of control. On Facebook, she had over 700 friend requests. Elva snapped shut her laptop. Her fanfic was a viral disaster. She was the target for global fanfic humiliation. Her story was crap, absolute total crap, and destined for GAFF (GodAwful Fanfic Forums). She was becoming a legend but not in a good way.

She tried to take a deep calming breath. The fabric of space time had warped. Fanfic hadn't brought her out of hell. No, what she was feeling was endless and fiery. Oh hell, fanfic had plunged her into hell.

She let her head fall forward, a dead weight on

her shoulders. Mitch had been right. He hadn't written comments on her manuscript to embarrass her, but to save her from this certain fate—Earth's Ultimate Loser Girl. Mitch was real. He'd put out his hand to lift her into Normal, and she'd walked away from the hottest kisses that had ever come her way.

Boiling explosions of humiliation rocketed through her like destructive space anomalies. Only the strongest and fittest survive in this world, Darwin's Theory and all. She stayed there, hunched over her laptop, wrapped up in a force field of pain. The ache reached deep into her bones. Her lifelines were useless. All of her yoga meditating and practicing had led her here. People were born to be what they had to be. They could never change. She was shooting for the moon, hoping to land in the stars, but instead here she was stuck in Podunk, Texas, learning her positiviness was like a kid playacting.

Papaw tapped on her bedroom door.

"Gal, we need to talk."

"About what?" Elva asked. She didn't get up.

"I called the Belling Meat Market today. They told me you called and cancelled. They got no plans to pick up the goats. What the heck is going on here?"

"I'm trying to save the goats," Elva said. "I don't want them to die."

"Why in the hell would you want to save them? They're nothing but walking meat."

He didn't understand anything, and she didn't think he ever would. She had to use her own words to tell him what the goats meant to her. It was the only option left.

"The kids, their lives continuing, are a sign that things will work out for me," Elva said.

"Humph." Papaw's face scrunched up.

"If the goats die, my hopes will die with them. I know it. Look at Nonny, her hope died when my mama died. Death kills hope. And you and Nonny won't be with me forever. Y'all are going to die too. And when you're gone, I'll be alone. I need to know the universe is on my side. The goats living are my sign."

"Now, why would you say something like that?" Papaw was upset.

"I'm telling you what I feel, what I need."

"I don't know what you're talking about. I do know I'm calling the Meat Market to get someone out to pick up these goats.

"Papaw, please, please, try to understand. Hear me." Elva couldn't help her voice breaking and her tears rolling.

"I'm trying, honey." He was shaking but he moved to cover it up by leaning against the door jam. "The goats are just meat. I don't understand your signs, your yogi power, but I do know I'm going be here for you as long as I'm here. And when I'm gone, hell, I'll join the angels to watch over you. And you have plumbing too; you can always fall back on plumbing. People always need a good plumber."

She could always fall back on plumbing.

Nonny joined Papaw at the doorway. "I've heard enough." She tapped Papaw's shoulder. "Pa, give her a week to save the dang goats."

"That don't make any sense to me," Papaw said.

"Hell, when has anything in this life ever made any sense?" Nonny asked.

Elva had never heard truer words.

Papaw was silent for a moment and then he nodded. "I'll give her a week but that's all I can tolerate."

A funny catch was in his voice and she saw glimmering in his eyes. He hurried to his bedroom and closed the door. He was as upset as she was, but no way was he shedding a tear in front of her. He was Old Texas, keeping his emotions tight and close was a law. Papaw had been shaped by hurricane force winds. He couldn't bend much more. The goats would be roasts in a week if she didn't figure this out. The thought hurt, but Elva let the bitterness of it go and forgave him there and then. Papaw loved her in his way. For all his faults, he was a good soul.

"Don't pay him any mind. Things have a way of turning out bearable." Nonny wrapped Elva into a big soft hug, and Elva clung to her.

33 ONE MORE WEEK

The goats had one more week.

Nonny went to bed early. Papaw didn't come out of the bedroom again. Elva spent the time surfing the Internet searching for new ideas to keep her goat brethren alive. It was late when her phone rang. Startled, she almost fell off her chair. Her left leg had fallen asleep from sitting for so long.

"Hello." She answered her phone and hopped to her feet.

"I saw your blog," Mitch said. "Are you OK?"

She'd only posted her story last night. Stalker. She jumped up and down through painful prickling as the feeling came back in her leg. Why did he have to be so nice? He'd told her not to post, and here he was still caring. Elva's lip trembled, and she chanted her favorite old mantra.

"Being poor sucks. Accepting it is the path of peace." Her old mantra wasn't cutting it any more. Even with all her meditating and practicing yoga, here she was, set adrift.

"It does at that," Mitch said. "That stuff online was brutal. You didn't deserve most of it. Your story wasn't that bad. Are you sure you're OK?"

"I'm fine." Elva parsed her words carefully. She feigned Vulcan disinterest to avoid a spat of uncontrollable sobs. The fanfic humiliation had pummeled her, and then Papaw and the goats had knocked her down. It was way too much. "I'm good." She tried to keep her voice steady, but inside, she was shouting in English and Klingon— "Tell him you're a pile of road kill."

"You're not fine. Do you want me to come over?" he asked.

"Right now?"

"Right now. I'll be there in a half hour."

"In the middle of the night?" Elva said. "Papaw won't take kindly to it."

"Then don't tell him." Mitch said in his frank, open way.

"OK, but don't come in by the door," Elva said. "Come through my window. My light will be on."

"On my way."

Click. Mitch didn't say goodbye. Not even a hint of sweetheart, honey, or darling. But he was on his way, and that was beyond huge.

***

270

Elva powered down her computer and waited for him. Maybe she shouldn't have said yes. Should she call him and cancel? She couldn't do it. She needed a friend, somebody on her side.

Mitch pulled up in his Bronco a couple minutes shy of a half hour. Elva saw him turn off his lights out by the road. It was only a few seconds before he knocked softly at her window.

"It's open," Elva said.

Mitch climbed through and sat next to her on the bed. He tossed his flip-flops on the floor. He wore a crinkled t-shirt and running shorts. His hair stuck out in all directions, like he hadn't bothered to brush it before he left.

"Will we wake up your grandparents?" he asked.

"Not possible," Elva said. "They sleep like the dead."

"Good." Mitch stared at her in that intense way of his. His hands cupped her face, and he tilted it into the light from her beside lamp.

"Sweetie, you've been crying." His thumbs stroked her cheeks.

Elva pulled back and hugged her pillow. "Why do you keep after me? I broke a mirror and put a voodoo curse on you."

"I figured as much," Mitch said, "but I like you." He stretched out next to her on her bed, and rolled on his back with his knees bent. "I think I can take a voodoo curse."

Elva pinched his side. "Says the boy who cut off his nose in front of me."

He put a forearm over his face. "No girl should ever see a guy's nose off his face. It's not right."

"It wasn't pretty either." Elva reached out and tapped his nose. "But your plastic surgeon did wonders."

She giggled and Mitch grabbed her forearms and pulled her down beside him. She felt so normal. Not something she'd known a lot of. The light-hearted moment shifted when he fixed that arrow gaze on her again. His hair fell over the side of his face. The curving tips touched his lips. Elva smoothed the strands behind his ear. An unbidden tear slid across her nose.

"Talk to me. I'm a good listener." He rolled on his back again and stared up at the ceiling.

Elva rolled on her back too. They lay there, shoulder to shoulder, arm to arm, thigh to thigh. He smelled like outdoors, and the hairs on his leg were scratchy.

"Today was impossible," she said. "You know about the fanfic, but you don't know about the goats."

"So what's going on with your goat brethren?" He seemed so genuinely interested.

"Papaw wants to sell them for meat unless I can figure a place for them to go. I've tried everywhere and can't find anything. They must live. They're my sign."

"What do you mean?" Mitch's fingers interlaced

with hers.

"The world is so hostile. When I named the goats at the beginning of the summer, I did it because it gave me hope. Everything was freaking changing. I saw the goats, breathing, enduring, thriving—as my ultimate sign. If they lived, I'd know for sure good stuff was ahead for me. My soul links to signs. I'm made that way."

"Elva, I've never really believed in signs, but you make me want to." Mitch reached out and enveloped her in his embrace. His lips pressed against the top of her head. "I'm sorry you had such a hard day." The sound of his heart, strong and unending, thum bum, thum bum, washed away her tense feelings like a downpour scours away the dust of a drought.

"I'm sorry about the goats and that I ever said anything about your story." The vibrations of Mitch's voice resonated in her chest.

"I'm not. At least I listened to you about the grammar." Elva's lips brushed a button on his shirt. "A few people commented that the grammar was decent." She placed a hand on his ribcage. His framework was less compact than hers, spare and open. Strong.

"I'm glad to be of service." Mitch tapped Elva's back.

She rubbed her cheek against his chest. "I'm glad too."

They fit together, an indefinable cosmic pair.

"I'm not throwing my story away," she

whispered.

She felt him nod. "You're no quitter." His words worked deep, rooting into her heart.

"I'll salvage it."

"Good."

And it was good. So good. Her heart, his heart, her breathing, his breathing, both of them here in this moment, together; it was the thirst-slaking connection she hungered for. Mitch wasn't moving too fast or too slow. They had time. He was the best lifeline in the storms of life she'd ever grabbed. She didn't feel alone for once in her life. She'd not realized how holding onto a real person made you feel like you could face anything as long as you're together.

Neither spoke for a while.

"Did I mention my friend Shay is pregnant?" she asked, yawing. Sleepiness crept over her.

"You're kind of like a hurricane." Mirth laced Mitch's response.

"Why?" Elva asked.

"You're unpredictable and wild."

"You're calling me a hurricane because I said my friend Shay is pregnant?" Elva opened her eyes to find Mitch gazing at her. Their faces were so close she could see half moons of faint freckles under his eyes.

"That's the unpredictable part," Mitch said.

"And exactly what part of me is wild?" she asked.

"I'm not sure," Mitch said. "But I've got a

feeling."

And then he leaned in and kissed her—a slow lazy kiss—a pure, romantic kiss—a perfect kiss.

"So will you go with me to my friend Margarett's wedding next Saturday?" Elva asked.

Mitch took his sweet time. He tucked her face into her neck and drummed his fingers on her back. Finally, he said, "I guess, but that's enough talk. Why don't you rest?"

Elva wanted to holler for joy. Tingles swarmed over her back and shoulders, and it struck her, this was the same feeling she had every time Kirk said, " … to explore strange new worlds, to seek out new life and new civilization, to boldly go where no man has gone before."

She snuggled next to Mitch and followed his breathing, matching her breaths with his and drifted off.

When Elva woke up in the morning, Mitch was gone.

A note was on her nightstand. It read, *I will see you next Saturday in the morning*.

34 MARGARETT'S WEDDING

She and Mitch each had big work weeks, so Elva really didn't see him until just before the wedding. She talked to him twice on her cell phone, but he wasn't one for chit-chat.

On Saturday, she woke early, did her nails, and rolled her hair. Then she pulled on the puffy pink bridesmaid dress that she'd bought at Maria Magdalena's Bridal Warehouse. Her worst fears were realized when she caught a glimpse of herself in the living room mirror. She looked precisely like a snowball cupcake sprinkled with hot-pink dyed coconut. The black velvet portrait of Elvis reflected in the mirror over her shoulder. She turned and stuck out her tongue at it.

"Who are you looking at?"

And then she went out to feed the goats. She

scooped feed into their trough. No more bottles, they were done. On Monday the butcher was coming. She'd called everywhere and nothing had turned up. No one would take the kids. It didn't make any sense, but she still hadn't given up on them. She wouldn't. Not until there was no hope.

Mitch pulled up in front of the house, got out of his truck and leaned against the hood. He gave her a long check-you-out stare. Elva rubbed her bare feet in the dirt and scratched goat sister Christine's sleek neck. The puffy dress billowed around them like a cloud.

"Yum," he said.

"I know. I look like a giant snowball cupcake."

Mitch was beside her in an instant and his hot cinnamon-ny breath brushed her cheek. How in the heck had he moved that fast?

"I don't think being a cupcake is a bad thing." His deep voice sent a cascade of chills down her back. He dropped a kiss on her bare shoulder, pulling up a sleeve that had slipped down.

"I'll go in and get my shoes." Elva's voice faltered and she took a step back. An unwanted blush rushed to her face.

Mitch smiled. "I'll wait for you in the truck."

She hurried in the house and put on the horrendous dyed-to-match shoes. She grabbed a bag with a change of clothes. A metamorphosis from cupcake into a normal girl would happen as soon as the ceremony was over.

"I'll see you in a while," Nonny said as Elva

headed out the door. "Papaw's driving me to the wedding."

Elva nodded and hopped outside, letting the screen door snap shut. At the truck, Mitch reached across the cab and opened the door for her. Soon they were turning into the Holiness parking lot.

Elva greeted Shay standing on the porch.

"We need to hurry," Shay said. "We have to put up our hair."

Elva gave Mitch a questioning look.

"You go on," Mitch said. "I've got a book to read. I'll be on the bride's side when the wedding starts."

Elva followed Shay to the back of the church. In a small room, Margarett's four aunts and mom bustled with bobby pins, brushes, and hairspray.

Margarett sat at a makeshift dressing table. Her hair was done up in a serious bun the size of a giant cinnamon roll. Her wedding dress was white satin covered with lace, ill-fitting, but modest, dang it. There were rows and rows of frills, quadruple more than Elva's ball of pink puffy fluff. These Pentecostals sure went all out for weddings.

"My wedding starts in an hour," Margarett said. "You're so late, Elva."

"Hey, chill, Margarett," Shay said. "This is your wedding day. Enjoy it." Shay smoothed down her dress, the satin sheath in snowball cupcake pink to match Elva's. Her dress was loose because she'd lost weight from the morning sickness. Elva's dress was loose too, but no one would notice with the masses of bows and frills. It didn't matter. This was

Margarett's day. God help her.

Elva plopped down on a stool next to Shay, and Margarett's aunts moved in to twist and curl their hair. One aunt scraped Elva's hair into a bun so tight the sides of her face were pulled back. Shay didn't have enough hair for a bun so they pinned on a fake one. Elva reviewed the final result in the cracked mirror. She looked like a chubby Barbie doll with a muffin glued to her head.

"Time for make-up!" Shay said.

The aunts and Margarett's mother took horrified breaths. Elva gave a mournful shake of her head at the unending Pentecostal nonsense.

"I'm not wearing make-up," Margarett said. "It's unseemly."

Shay stared at Margarett and then said, "Let me take care of that zit. It's your wedding day."

Margarett had a huge red zit on the side of her nose.

"I've got my concealer," Shay said, "No one will notice."

Margarett looked at her mama. "It's my wedding."

Margarett's mama looked like she was about to throw a hissy fit. A person could go to Hell for wearing make-up in Pentecostal land, but she suddenly relaxed.

A miracle!

"All right," she said. "For your wedding."

"Hallelujah, there is a God!" Shay dotted Margarett's zit with her concealer and began to blend it. "It seems like yesterday that we were in the cafeteria writing those crazy *Star Trek* stories with Elva." Shay stood back and admired her handiwork. The concealer really did help Margarett's looks.

"I can't believe it, either," Margarett said, as her mother tucked a white rose into the massive bun on the back of her head.

"Yeah," Elva said, contemplating this new state of affairs that relegated *Star Trek* fanfic to the backwaters of their history.

One of Margarett's aunts handed a bouquet of white roses to Margarett and then handed ribbon decorated tambourines to Shay and Elva. Hundreds of pink and white satin ribbons had been tied to the rims. "We decided these tambourines would suit you girls as well as flowers," her aunt said.

Elva looked down at the tambourine. Did they expect her to play it?

"Just rattle it when everybody claps," Margarett said. Elva glanced at her, grateful for the explanation and yet horrified at the same time. She gave Shay her Spock eyebrow, and they both giggled.

"Y'all squeeze together and let me get a picture." Margarett's grandma came in with a camera.

Elva, Shay, and Margarett obliged. They smooshed together and grinned wide. The sound of the "Wedding March" flooded the small room.

It was time.

Shay went first, and Elva followed, hooking arms with Margarett's younger brother. He was two inches shorter than her and stick thin. Elva stepped into the sanctuary of Holiness. Mitch was halfway up the aisle on the bride's side. Nonny and Papaw were next to him. He seemed more than fine holding his Catalina hat in hand, tall and thin, with slicked back hair and shiny black boots. He smiled at her encouragingly as she passed.

Up front, Chase waited for Margarett. He came across almost handsome in his white tux with tails. Elva took her place beside Shay. Everyone clapped when Margarett began her march up the aisle. Elva gave her tambourine the obligatory rattle.

After an hour long sermon about the virtues of the Pentecostals, the glory of tongue speaking, and the importance of holiness, Margarett and Chase were married.

Everyone piled in their cars for the reception. It was almost an hour's drive from Belling. Chase's family was throwing it out of town to keep down gossip. There would be alcohol (champagne to toast the bride) and dancing.

The Holiness crowd planned to boycott the whole thing at first because it gave an appearance of evil. Alcohol was the devil's drink. And dancing? A sure slide into Hell. Elva had snorted soda out her nose when she heard that.

Nonny and Papaw took Shay to the reception because understandably she didn't have a date, being pregnant and all. Elva went with Mitch. She asked him to stop at the first McDonalds.

"Do you want a soda?" Mitch asked.

"Oh, you are reading my mind," Elva said. She grabbed her trash bag of clothing and headed into the restroom. She pulled on blue jeans and a t-shirt and shoved her dress into the bag. Elva quickly put color around her eyes. The eyeliner brought out the golden lights. She'd forgotten her tennis shoes and had to keep wearing the pink heels. Mitch grinned when she wobbled back to the Bronco. He handed her a Diet Coke.

"Nice shoes."

They both laughed, and then Elva chatted about the ridiculous wedding for a while as Mitch drove. He answered with monosyllabic words: yeah, right, good, and he nodded a lot. He just wasn't one for words. Eventually, they fell into an easy silence.

The reception was being held at an obscure Masonic lodge off the highway. As they slowed on the off-ramp, the sun shone in her eyes. Elva blinked rapidly and looked away. The moment her focus returned; something flipped in her stomach. A weathered sign hung on a fence post at the end of the exit ramp. It read 'Goat Sanctuary' and an arrow pointed up the road. There was a phone number, too.

She dialed the number and in minutes it was all settled.

The wailing part of the *Star Trek* theme rose inside her. She threw back her head. Waves of laughter shook her. Three picayune goats were destined to have a life. Finally, she'd found a place for them to live without a worry. Much of life seemed all noise and rage, tearing up people and taking them away, but she knew that in this moment she was fulfilling a calling. She'd fought against the unseen and carved out a place for the babies.

Confidence welled up in her. She'd done the impossible, something that didn't have a hope or a prayer. Who knew how many impossible things were ahead?

"Good news?" Mitch asked.

Tears of relief and joy leaked from her eyes. "We're really in control of our destiny."

"I wondered when you were going to figure that out," Mitch said.

Mitch didn't have many words, but ones he did have were certainly comforting.

35 MORE

A couple of days later, Elva handed over three crisp one hundred dollar bills to the goat sanctuary man. McCoy, M'Benga, and Nurse Christine Chapel were saved.

Elva kissed each smooth nose before the goat man loaded them into his trailer.

Nonny joined her outside to watch the trailer pull away. "I'll miss the kids."

"I will, too." Elva gave Nonny a squeeze.

Goat saving, Elva's ultimate sign, was complete. Margarett would call it the Holy Spirit's providence. Shay would call it the power of positive thinking. On *Star Trek* they would call it a singularity or cosmic phenomena. Elva took it as excellent karma.

"I'm glad you saved the goats." Nonny patted

Elva's shoulder. "I'm going up to Wal-Mart to buy shoes for my new job. Do you want to come with?" Nonny had gotten a call from Belling Elementary. One of the lunch ladies had quit, and Nonny got the job with full benefits. Another miracle.

"I'll stay here." Elva said, stretching. "School starts on Monday, and I want to sit under the water sprinkler at least once. I haven't had a chance all summer."

Nonny left and Elva sprawled in a lawn chair under the whizz-whizz of sweeping water. She watched the rainbows flashing in each arc. The cicadas hummed and crows chattered. The wind was hot on her face. She picked at the calluses on her palms, revealing the pink skin underneath, and lifted her hair, enjoying the spray of water against her neck.

Life wasn't just a series of disasters as she'd once thought. Life was an endless adventure. Maybe she'd be a writer. Maybe *Star Trek* was her destiny. Or maybe not. Elva remembered her resolve when Mitch cut off his nose. Blood didn't make her a bit queasy. Perhaps she'd be an EMT or a doctor.

Dr. Elva Presley Hicks.

It had a nice ring to it, just like Dr. Leonard McCoy.

Lord, she was glad plumbing was over, but she wasn't sad she'd done it. Plumbing had taught her to chart her own life, and why the heck not. The summer had burned every bit of yellow-bellied cowardice out of her. The future beckoned. Mitch wanted her to go to Lone Star College with him. The stack of money in her account put that within reach. Her old mantra came to mind: Being poor sucks. Accepting it is the pathway of peace.

It was not longer her truth. She'd have to find a new one.

Who knew plumbing would beam her out of small town hell?

She looked down at her trimmed thighs and less poochy belly. Weight loss was something she could get used to. She leaned back in the lawn chair and let the sun soak into her skin. The power energized her bones. She took a deep cleansing breath and slowly exhaled. All of her yoga practice led to this moment, one of absolute true consciousness.

She was enough.

Later, her phone buzzed—a text from Shay.

Bring the fanfic on Monday.

Another buzz followed—a text from Margarett.

Don't you dare forget it!

A third buzz. Who could it be now?

Chase.

I'm in for fanfic. Let's add an engineering tech who boosts the efficiency of the Bussard ramscoop.

Did they want a tech nut in their group? Elva thought.

Margarett texted immediately.

Honey, of course you can join us. You're so deep.

Shay texted.

Sure.

Elva grumbled. Apparently, Chase Fleaso was a

new fixture in the Loser Girl club.

She texted the group.

Chase can join only if he swears to never, never, never include anything about the Enterprise series.

Her phone immediately buzzed. Chase.

I swear.

And it was done. Chase was trekking with them.

On Monday, Elva hurried to the bus stop, managing to bypass the powdered donuts Nonny had left on the kitchen table. She didn't want to jeopardize the usability of her new jeans—junior size 17!—and a cherry t-shirt from a trendy clothing store at the mall—size XL!—too tight, but in a good way.

It was already blazing hot before school. The weather man had predicted well over a hundred for the first day of her senior year in Hell (oh, the joy of high school). The yellow dog bus ride over the river Styx was uneventful. Jolie and Dylan were making out. Their baby snoozed in his car seat. Jolie came up for air as Elva sat on the opposite seat.

"Wow, Elva, you've lost weight," Jolie said and turned back to the hicky fest on Dylan's neck. He didn't speak. Elva had never been certain if he had higher functioning abilities. Her eyes narrowed. Dylan was definitely a child of Risa (that sexy *Star Trek* planet). Maybe she'd work him and Jolie into her next story.

Elva passed on the cinnamon rolls in the cafeteria. She was determined to not give in to sugar-coated landmines.

Yes, Star Trek fanfic was on. She joined the Loser Girls plus Chase at their table by the window and slapped down the current pages.

"Being pregnant sure itches." Shay scrubbed at her belly as she sat down next to Elva, "And I'm starved all the time. Can I have the rest of your cereal?"

Elva offered her the paper bowl. "You're feeding two."

Margarett pressed her hand to her face as the milk sloshed. She ran out of the lunch room.

Chase Fleaso smiled. "I guess you're not the only one having a baby. We're due sometime late April."

His face was beaming.

The Belling High School Daycare would be expanding this year. Elva wanted to close her eyes and scream. Instead, she shuffled to class, willfully ignoring the wolf whistles and appreciative glances.

At the end of the day, she waved goodbye to her friends. Chase offered her a ride home, but she had a ride and waited on the grass by the bronze Texas Ranger statue donated to Belling High by the class of '82.

When Mitch pulled into the parking lot, Elva waved. He gave her a long slow smile. There were at least fifty faces pressed up to the long windows in the cafeteria.

"Want to go for a drive?" He reached across the seat and opened the door for her.

"Sure." She climbed in, aware that dozens of kids had their heads hanging out of their bus windows, watching the miracle of Elva Presley Hicks leaving school with a halfway decent guy.

"Where do you want go?" he asked.

"Out to the Gulf," she answered.

"Sure enough, darlin'."

He didn't ask her why. She didn't have to explain anything to him, not one word about how she needed to connect with her mom, and since her mom's ashes were scattered in the Gulf that's where she had to go.

They drove south on the backroads to the coast, not speaking as they passed through acres of rice paddies and occasional small towns.

When they came into Freeport, Mitch asked, "Are you hungry?"

"No, I just want a Diet Coke."

He turned into the Sonic and ordered. "I want a medium Dr Pepper and a medium Diet Coke with cherry syrup."

"I didn't say anything about cherry," Elva said.

"I thought you'd like it."

"I would, but you could've asked." Elva folded her arms.

"I didn't ask because I know you."

How was she going to argue with that? They sipped their drinks, and Mitch headed toward the water, the sun low on the horizon. He drove the Bronco along the packed beach until he found a place without many cars. They stopped, facing the rows of low dunes with blue-green lines of tufted salt grass along the peaks. Elva pulled off her shoes and socks and hopped out. A few screaming gulls wheeled overhead. Mitch circled around and leaned against the tailgate. She followed. Soft sand slid like hot silk on her soles.

Mitch's arms were crossed and his hat hung low, covering his eyes. He held out a hand, and pulled Elva between his legs. His chest was almost too warm against her back, and she felt his sweat seeping into her cotton tee.

He took her hand into his own; his lips close to her ear.

"I haven't read your love line yet."

"You haven't." The heat of a blush rose in her cheeks.

"Let me see." He slowly traced the line across her palm. "You're a romantic, full of warmth and spice. You fight for those you love at all costs."

His arms slid around her waist, anchoring her to him.

"Does it really say that?"

"If it doesn't, it should."

His smile curved against her temple. Neither of them said another word. They watched the splashing waves of the Gulf, and the sun's gleaming orange path on the wet sand. A lone thunderhead hung low on the horizon and broke the light into shafts that splayed in all directions. Elva was sure if she gazed straight into the sun as it sank, she'd see Willa Jo standing at those pearly gates, smiling down at her.

36 KARMA

Elva had been so lost in her memories she almost missed the Jersey Village exit. It was hard to believe it had been almost six years since that summer. Her time with Mitch had been pure magic, but like the last original *Star Trek* movie, she headed to the undiscovered country in the end. The summer after high school, Mitch transferred to Texas A&M for construction science and she enrolled at U of H. They broke up and lost touch.

Life happened.

She followed the GPS instructions to Margarett's apartment.

Margarett was getting dressed. One of her cousins was in the kitchen and planned to babysit. Elva sat on the couch with Dreama and Cory. Margarett had two children before she and Chase split a year after high school.

"The tooth fairy left me five whole dollars," Dreama said, showing off her missing front teeth. Cory sidled up to Elva and put his arms around her.

"You smell nice," he said. He was even pinker than his daddy.

Margarett came out of the bedroom. She wore a cute blue mini that matched the electric blue tips on her short bob haircut.

"Gosh, I'm ready for a night of dancing. Give me a kiss, loves." Dreama and Cory jumped off the couch, and then Margarett and Elva headed out.

The party barge at Lake Conroe was lit up like a Christmas tree. A text from Shay popped up.

Meet me at the bar.

They found her with a cute guy by her side.

"Do you remember my date?" Shay asked.

Elva squinted. His blue eyes twinkled. He looked kind of familiar. Dear God, was it Kyle? He'd thrown a tampon at them once.

"Hi, Elva," Kyle said. "I hope nothing I did in high school still troubles you. I've gotten the Lord since, and I'm sorry for all that."

He'd moved past his freak-show stage and had turned into a catch.

"Kyle is a youth minister at our church," Shay gushed.

Good for Shay, Elva thought. Shay'd given up her baby for adoption while in high school, and then her mom had died in a wreck the following

Christmas. Bliss needed to flood Shay's life.

"It's funny how things work out," Elva said.

Shay nodded as the "Cotton-eyed Joe" began playing over the loud speakers.

"Let's go!" Shay said. "Stomp, kick, and triple step!"

Elva linked arms with her friends and they joined the other dancers.

They danced until sweat was running down her cheeks, and then, on the way to the restroom, Elva's world turned upside down.

She brushed past one of the boat staffers and was shocked when his hand gripped her arm.

"Elva?"

She'd never forget that gravelly voice. Mitch.

"What are you doing here?" Elva asked. Mitch's shoulders were wider and his hair shorter, but his eyes were the same, warm honey and cheerful.

"I finished at A&M, and I'm working in Houston again. Tonight, I'm helping my cousin. He owns the boat." Mitch took a step back.

"You must have known I'd be here. This is my class reunion." Elva gave him her Spock eyebrow for old time's sake.

Mitch blushed. "I've wondered what you've been up to. This seemed like a good time to check in. Are you still writing your fanfic?"

"Funny thing you should ask," Elva said." I haven't thought about it in years, but just today it came back to me. I'm going to give it another go."

"You're no quitter." His hand gripped hers and

she felt that cosmic connection with him again. "Meet me up top later. I go off shift at ten."

"I'll think about it."

Elva joined Shay and Margarett at the bar. She ordered a drink and munched on the spicy pretzels.

"You won't believe who I ran into," Elva said.

"Who," Shay asked.

"Mitch McCall."

Margarett spit a mouthful of beer. "What are you doing with us then?"

"He doesn't get off shift until ten." Elva said, sipping her rum and coke.

"This is one time you need to boldly go," Margarett said.

"For sure." Shay added. "Mitch was the best thing that ever happened to you."

"On behalf of Loser Girl kind, I demand you find out if there is something more there," Margarett shook her blue-tipped curls.

"It could be a blessing from the Lord," Shay said.

Elva laughed at that. Go figure, Shay would go all religion on them.

"I'll do it," Elva said, lifting her glass. "For Loser Girl kind."

All three laughed together and clinked their glasses.

A little after ten, Elva left the dance floor and headed up the ladder to the topside of the party barge.

Mitch was waiting.

His eyes lit up as he stretched out a hand. She

took it, and they waltzed across the roof, stars twinkling overhead.

She was breathless when they finally stopped by the wood railing. Elva could see Margarett and Shay below, waving up. Shay lifted an eyebrow and tilted her head at Mitch. Margarett winked. Elva flashed a "live long and prosper" sign to them both. They cheered and raised the sign back to her.

Mitch's arm slid around her waist, pulling her to him.

"Might as well give them a show."

He tipped up her chin and kissed her. Peppermint and lime.

Elva's lips curved. A higher power was at work. The future was making up for every ounce of crap that had ever come her way. She reached for the railing and knocked on wood. This is what the road of absolutely normal felt like.

In this moment, she realized some greatness of the Universe had seeped inside her. She had become more. Above her, a shooting star streaked across the mystery swath of diamond lights embedded in blue velvet. Elva smiled as the brilliant trail disappeared as quickly as it came. She could feel herself going with the infinite possibilities.

The Universe was smiling on her for sure.

ACKNOWLEDGMENTS

Thanks to Suzanne Wetterman Bahm, Margaret Mingolo Degange, and Susan Melenkevitz Haven for auld lang syne.

Many writers helped me during the creation of this book. There is no way to mention everyone, but special thanks to: Cathy Benson, Conrad Wesselhoeft, Peggy King Anderson, Katherine Grace Bond, Kathy Whitehead. Kevan Atteberry, Megan Bilder, Judy Bodmar, Vijaya Bodach, Janet Lee Carey, Robin Cox, Holly Cupala, Karen K. Dunn, Chris Eboch, Susan Greenway, Marion Holland, Jen Heger, Ellen McGinty, Allyson Valentine Schrier, Shelley Seely, Andy Sherrod, Louise Spiegler, and Stasia Kehoe Ward.

Also, thank you to SCBWI for awesome support, especially the Martha Weston Grant Committee and the Hairston family for their belief in my work. Special thanks to Liz Mertz for the gifts of editing.

Finally, thanks to my family. To my aunt and uncle, Angie and Roger Wright, for their unfailing support. To my sisters, Angie Broussard and Lee Ann Barlow Kuruganti, for sharing my journey. To my dad, Jack Barlow, for teaching me to work hard, and to my mom, Lera Lee Kelly Barlow, I wish you could have read this book. I also thank my awesome kids— Josiah, Jubilee, Jesse and Jack. Y'all are the best. Last of all, thanks to the love of my life, Timothy.

ABOUT THE AUTHOR

Cece Barlow writes books for young adults and the young at heart. She's a dash of fun, mixed in with some smart cookie and a splash of capable. She started her first fan fiction group in junior high and never stopped writing. Today, she writes about strange worlds, girls with lofty dreams and the absolute craziness of falling love.

When Cece's not writing, she curls up with a book, heads to a popcorn blockbuster, or kicks back to watch shooting stars. If she sees the moon in the daytime, she thinks she's lucky. Cece lives in College Station, Texas with her college sweetheart Tim and two cats - one evil and one good.

For more info: cecebarlow.blogspot.com.

Made in the USA
Lexington, KY
12 May 2019